D1491947

THE FOURTH OF JUNE

Eton, with its totems and taboos, is a difficult place for a boy without the instinct to conform or the background to understand. Scarfe had neither — he was a guinea-pig. Until the doctor had to be called, there seemed no reason why the Captain of the House at Manningham's should not be left to make a gentleman of him.

THE FOURTH
OF JUNE

David Benedictus

THE BOOK CLUB
121 CHARING CROSS ROAD
LONDON, W.C.2

First published in June, 1962 by
Anthony Blond Ltd

PRINTED IN GREAT BRITAIN
BY EBENEZER BAYLIS AND SON, LTD.
THE TRINITY PRESS, WORCESTER, AND LONDON

CONTENTS

For my parents
who deserve better

AUTHOR'S NOTE: It is inevitable in a book of this kind that some lonely person somewhere will imagine himself portrayed. Let me therefore emphasize that it has not been my intention to portray anyone, lonely or otherwise, that care has been taken to avoid such portrayals, and that all characters in the book, including those holding official positions, are entirely imaginary. The incidents described did not, so far as I know, happen, but I can see no reason, if they did not, why they did not.

Things have changed since I was at Eton. College Chapel has a new roof and three more stained-glass windows. The 'scugger' is no longer much in evidence and the scaffolding is gone from the cloisters. There is talk of a bypass. There was talk, too, at the Headmasters' Conference, of implementing the very few vacancies for poorer boys from government schools, talk which may yet, through the foresight of Dr. Robert Birley, Headmaster of Eton, and Sir Desmond Lee, Headmaster of Winchester, and in spite of the thick-headedness of councils and such, be translated into action.

Things have changed, but I don't believe that Etonians have. Younger brothers, and soon eldest sons, will carry on the traditions of snobbery and cruelty unless . . . Unless what? Good luck and eloquence to Dr. Birley and Sir Desmond Lee!

David Benedictus, 1962

PART ONE

CHAPTER ONE

'BLOODY funny Bishop, that Bishop,' said Pemberton.

'He is a Bishop,' replied Morgan, 'what more can we expect?'

'Fine pair of shoulders on him, though. Godlike shoulders. Good sin-bearing shoulders, I should think. How are your sins today, Phillips? Weighing you down?'

Phillips crossed his legs. Nowadays he seemed to be all knees; he couldn't make the simplest movement without them obtruding. But it was ridiculous to be so self-conscious where knees were concerned.

So Confirmation Class had been its usual farcical self, nobody in earnest except Scarfe and – presumably – the Bishop. He was glad he had had the guts to cut it when he had. 'Course it was all fine for those lucky enough to have something to be confirmed in, but he had said specifically that he wouldn't be confirmed, and so he hadn't, and wouldn't . . . And yet it would have been nice to have had a faith. Big word, faith. Big Bishop too. But faith in what? Humanity? Look about you, lad, look about you. It might be all right for those brought up on *Lives of the Saints* and *The Water Babies* and such, but he had always preferred Hans Andersen, and, come to think of it, still liked the picture of the Marsh King's daughter . . . Humanity? Possibly. And then he looked at the faces of the other two, Morgan, dark and aquiline with sinister, almost hooded eyes, and Pemberton, fair and sharp-nosed and foxy. The eagle and the fox. Was there a fable about them in La Fontaine, he wondered. But why did *they* go to Confirmation Class, what did *they* believe in?

'How are your sins today, Phillips? Weighing you down?'

'No, I'm bearing up okay.' There was 'Le Renard et le

Corbeau', but in that the fox came out on top (always did in La Fontaine) and Pemberton could never . . .

'Why don't you go to Confirmation Class any more?' Pemberton was very inquisitive this evening. It was towards the end of March and the three of them were sitting in a small, square room with a sour smell and an ungenerous fire spluttering in the grate. The fire was Pemberton's, although the coal was shared, so he must have considered himself privileged to ask the questions. This time he didn't wait for an answer.

'You should have been there tonight. The Bishop was in civvies and had forgotten to fasten a fly. That made me feel truly religious.'

'Wouldn't take much to convert you then,' murmured Morgan.

'So I sort of smiled at him and told him "Star in the East" – you know, to show the old sod – and he beamed at me like a moron and said: "Aha, I see we have a mystic in our midst." Mystic! Huh! Smoke, anyone?'

Some of it true probably. But if it hadn't been his fly it would have been something else. Anything was grist for Pemberton's mill. And did Pemberton really feel that way? Or was he being clever? For instance did he . . . well did he ever kiss his mother?

'Pemberton, what's your mother like?'

'Oh, not your type at all, Phillips. Terribly, terribly not. Just not made for you. Utterly, utterly ravishing, of course, but, alas!, utterly, utterly ravished.' Pemberton was getting into his stride, and they would be lucky to learn anything now. 'She's like a fairy princess to me. Sometimes, late at night, when she's going to a dance, she comes into my room in her long black dress, her lovely white shoulders—'

'—glowing like candlelight on old silver—' Morgan couldn't let that opportunity pass.

'—to ruffle my hair and kiss me good night . . .' Pemberton's imagination was running dry so he burst into simulated sobs and laid his head on Morgan's lap. Morgan stroked his forehead and crooned soothingly to him. Phillips was embarrassed. You never knew with Morgan.

But what *was* his mother like? Phillips was very curious, he didn't know why he was so curious, to know. And what had Pemberton been like at seven, or five, or eighteen months. Maybe Morgan would know. You never knew with Morgan.

'How long have you known him, Morgan?'

'Generations,' said Morgan, and got up to fetch an ashtray.

'Don't leave me, don't leave me,' Pemberton called out, and clung to his coat-tails, like a widow to a bailiff's.

'Grow up,' said Morgan sternly. Pemberton let go at once, and this time he felt uncomfortable as well as Phillips. Having fetched the ashtray and asserted himself, Morgan relented.

'I first saw him at a gymkhana,' he said.

'There I was, pride of the community, and especially of my father, the Squire. Mater was not, as I recall, present at the time, having made up her mind (if her mind entered into it) after sixteen years of hesitation, to sleep with the second footman.' To both Morgan and Phillips this, however facetiously phrased, was beginning to sound at least like a possibility. 'Alas, how disappointed she was! Sixteen years of hesitation had proved too much for the poor man. But, like I said, there was Daddy, beaming all over his face, taking it like an officer and gentleman. He was ruddy good at taking it too. Years of practice.'

'If the British are good at anything, it's at taking it,' said Morgan.

'Oh ah. Rule Britannia. Well, I took every jump like a

veteran. Clipped a couple of bricks off a wall, but Daddy just smiled at the judges. Winningly. And, as I led my cobbled mare into the unsaddling enclosure, Lady Chalmers gave me quite a cut across the withers with her crop and muttered: "Clumsy bugger!" under her breath, slipping me a scented billet-doux still warm with the fragrance of her lily-white breast.'

Morgan was smiling like a ventriloquist at a forward dummy, a little ruefully, a little dangerously.

'Nothing but a load of cock,' he said and flung himself on Pemberton. The two of them were almost boyish in these nightly struggles on the floor, and they laughed a lot as they fought, but there was a terribly serious meaning to their fights if Phillips could only understand it, for he had often noticed certain signs . . . But he didn't understand, he couldn't hope to understand, and tonight he felt sick of the whole wretched business, whatever it was. Sick of their mockery, sick of their crudity, and sick too of the grace and flow of their eloquence.

He made his way along the dreary, surgical corridor and up the stairs towards his room. It was quite cold and yet, as always, the walls were sweating. The balustrade was sticky to the touch. He caught the flapping sole of his right shoe on the top stair, almost tripped – his knees went all ways at once – and put his hand to the wall to save himself with such force that his finger-nails went purple and white and the moons shone out. He must get his shoe mended, he thought, but of course he wouldn't. For the want of a nail . . . He must also see Scarfe when he got back from Confirmation Class, if it wasn't too late. Scarfe had got plenty of faith and to spare, but it wouldn't do to be seen talking to Scarfe too frequently during the daytime.

God, his room was untidy. There would be trouble about that if She had been snooping. As She probably had, looking for dirty books most likely, so She could give her stern but understanding Purity Lecture. She must be the world authority on Purity by now: when She pried into dusty corners of dusty rooms, the pages of magazines and books curled and shrivelled, fell to ashes under her burning eye-glass.

Phillips unhooked his bed from the wall and let it fall slowly into place. It lay unevenly, ruining the cover of a Marten and Carter. There were smudges on his wall where he had tried to erase some silly graffiti, pencilled up probably by Berwick in an excess of good-humour. There was still an inch or two of grey, soapy water in his wash-basin and some of it had slopped over the side and was dripping on to an old *Daily Express* on the floor. He could smell the wet newspaper. A special *Daily Express* smell. He opened the window, replaced the wedge, and could hear, suddenly, the lonely, crepuscular sound of birds gliding in from Datchet. A cracked voice echoed down the passage; 'Bugger you, Parsons, you wog!' Screams and curses. A scraping noise on the floor of the room above.

Sometimes he loathed Eton and everything to do with it.

Scarfe walked slowly back from Confirmation Class full of the love of God. He was also full of love for the Bishop. Not one of those self-important Anglican ecclesiasts that he had always been liable to meet on preaching missions in East Anglia (looking suddenly over hedges with cheery waves of manicured hands) full of their message, not The Message – but surely a modern saint. Everyone knew about his work in the Liverpool Boys' Clubs, and his brave – but liberal – broadcast speeches. Too good for this world, but this world could never be too wicked for him. And then he knew so much about his, Scarfe's, personal problems.

'Don't despise the Tempter,' he had said, 'and respect the temptations. How else can you hope to wrestle with them? Respect them. Seek them out. The traitor at the gate of the citadel is more dangerous than a whole arsenal of guns. Did you bring your collection box?'

Oh, he would wrestle with them all right; he would strain every sinew. There was so much in the world worth fighting for. Two jacketed lower-boys, on a fagging errand perhaps, pushed past him, scuffling. They were so young, thought Scarfe, they were enchanting. He would make his greatest efforts for them, and for the millions like them, who, not only in Britain, but . . . He began to hum. Maybe he himself would go into the Church, become a purple bishop, and spread the wonderful message. His message which would be *The* Message. What was it he was humming?

> If I have done my duty as a Christian ought,
> Then my living will not be in vain.

An honest unashamed song that had made him uncomfortable in the past, but what was there to be uncomfortable about now that his mind was made up and his conscience clear? A double cherry was bright with blossom in the garden of one of the masters. He sang over the chorus, right out loud, half-way along Judy's Passage with quite uncharacteristic defiance. He looked round him nervously, but there was no one (except, of course, Jesus) watching him. In spite of his ardour he was happy to find himself (comparatively) alone.

Scarfe was an odd-looking person. Short, even stunted, but with a thickness of trunk and legs that gave an impression, not of power, not of flabbiness, but of soundness; rather comic purposefulness. His head and neck were too small for his body – by the accepted proportions – like a chocolate soldier whose head a child has been sucking; the mirror need only be slightly distorted to show 'the

Great Panjandrum himself with a little round button at top'. He was, had become recently, rather sensitive about his appearance and his expression was apologetic. Sometimes people teased him about it. And, if it wasn't that they teased him about, it was surely something else.

He strutted very close to the strutted wooden fence on one side of the footpath; a habit of his. When they had told him about it, and had asked him why he did it, there hadn't been much he could say. Once, with a touch of intended humour, he had answered them: 'I'm afraid of thunderbolts,' and had been universally ridiculed for it. Perhaps if they had been trained to laugh at him or if it had become a part of their nature, there was nothing he could have said which would have made any difference. So that recently he had taken to walking down the exact centre of every path, passageway and corridor that he came to, but now his mind was on other things.

Scarfe was full of the love of God, but right now there didn't seem much that he could do about it; he had just been exhorted in general terms to feed the hungry, clothe the naked and set the captives free, which is all very well in the Bible, or in the mouth of a bold bishop, but in a Public School where would he find the naked or the hungry? And, as to captives, their parents (or guardians) were paying for their captivity, so they were hardly galley-slaves chained to their oars. Or cricket-bats.

Of course up till now they hadn't listened to him at all, laughed at him a lot, which they were welcome to do, he added to himself defiantly, but that was before he had this fire of Christ in him. Well maybe not quite that yet. But it would come. What was it the Bishop had said about it?

'Now you must not expect a bolt from the blue, or tongues of flame – nowadays that would be an inconvenience as well as an inspiration eh, ha ha? No, for most of us, for myself when I was your age (and I was!) as well as for you today, faith is a slow process; like run-down batteries you must recharge yourselves with love, until the divine spark ignites your lives and sends you off on your true journey, all cylinders – em – firing and in top gear.'

For the moment he must be content with speaking to them patiently, with speaking for them to God hopefully, and with speaking of them to the Bishop frequently. And if he did something about his East-Anglian voice, they would be more tolerant of his universal opinions. He would start on Phillips that very night.

He climbed briskly up the two flights of stairs to Phillips's room (it was not yet supper-time), a purposeful, squat figure; nor did he cling to the banisters this evening, nor hug the outside wall, but took the exact centre of the staircase, and was not a bit afraid of thunderbolts.

'Does anyone know the one about the biology lecturer who asked his class how many positions of love-making there were?' It was a rhetorical question. 'Well, this voice at the back shouted out: "Twenty-seven," and the lecturer raised his eye-brows, and asked who could tell him what the first position was. And a girl in the front said: "The girl lies on her back with her legs apart, and the man lies between them"; and the voice from the back shouted: "Twenty-eight." '

Berwick laughed with the others, loud enough to be heard above the others. He had heard it before, a bit coarser, a bit better told, but it still struck him as funny, and he'd dearly have liked to have known what were the other positions. His mother would have told him with pleasure, but it would be painful to ask her. Still it wouldn't do, it just wouldn't do to show them his ignorance, especially since he was entertaining them in his room in order to impress them with his worldliness.

'How many shagging positions do you know of, Ravens-court?' he asked the humorist, a fat, flap-eared, unhappy boy, who had found vulgarity the quickest – and cheapest – way to popularity, and so, like Berwick, was in Debate. Debate, whose self-electing members by tradition kept discipline without setting an example, and whose debating activity was confined to subjects which would have caused the Mother of Parliaments to have drawn back her skirts for shame. It wasn't really much of a gamble Berwick was taking because they wouldn't think to turn it against him. Ravenscourt could not find the right reply. There wasn't one. He knew what was coming. There still wasn't anything he could have said.

'Oh, quite a few, I suppose,' said Ravenscourt casually. They all waited for Berwick; he had only to strike, and the wet, wriggling fish was in his hands. He struck.

'Describe them,' said Berwick.

Ravenscourt did his best, but his ignorance was obvious to everyone. Some of his wilder suggestions (elicited by a Berwick in full cry) were blatant and comically absurd to the youngest there. Berwick pressed home his advantage.

'A hell's keen lover you'd make,' he said, and the gong sounded for supper. Like bees returning to a hive they trooped downstairs, all buzzing at once as if to clear their heads for serious eating. Berwick found himself next to Ravenscourt in the queue for macaroni cheese.

'Berwick,' said Ravenscourt hesitantly. He was angry, but still hesitant. 'Do *you* know what the positions are?'

Berwick at bay: 'Why, you little sod!' The Dame, who was straining her ears for bad language as she dished out the supper, smiled grimly and bided her time. Ravenscourt's anger evaporated before the greater wrath of the other. It was the time for conciliation. He added: 'Because I wish you'd tell me them.'

'Oh, go and – drown yourself!' cried Berwick, restrain-

ing himself, however, and seized a plate of macaroni
cheese. It was a very small helping, and She looked at him
out of the tops of her eyes to see if he understood. As he
made his way to a table, a voice at his elbow whispered:
'Naughty!' It was not his conscience, it was Morgan.
Berwick ignored him and sat down. He was puzzled. This
wasn't the way things usually were. This wasn't the order
of things. He was not accustomed to having his authority
questioned in this way. After all he was universally liked
and respected. He had several friends in Pop, the Eton
Society, and drank with them as often as was seemly in
Tap. It was rumoured that he had already chosen the
material for his waistcoat – leopardskin. He was already
in Debate and would make the Library in no time. In a
smallish house he was accepted in all the splinter groups –
or considered he was, and how should he learn the
contrary? – but leader of none. He came and he went.
Everyone called him amiable ('an amiable thug'); only a
few in private thought him cold. He was wooed by those
who thought him worth it and ignored only by those who
couldn't aspire to him. He was feared by his enemies, and
he was regarded with apprehension even by his friends. He
was tall, broad, and blondly handsome. He knew his
onions. He was a card. But he was not a great thinker.

Between supper and prayers, which were conducted by
Manningham, the housemaster, there was a half-hour
interim, hardly long enough it might be thought to change
from the physical to the spiritual, so most of the boys did
not bother, but contented themselves with being there,
which was compulsory, and with omitting to recite the
Lord's Prayer, which was not. But tonight Scarfe's 'Amens'
at least were magnificent. After prayers was the Business
of the Day; on this occasion merely an admonition against
the carving of names on the lavatory walls.

'If you wish to behave like savages,' Manningham

intoned, sighing at the Holy Scriptures in his hand as if they were the offenders, 'you must be treated like savages. Anyone caught carving their names will be savagely treated.' He walked to the door, and the boys rose, by tradition, to see him out. At the door he turned back, sighed again and added wearily: 'Anyone caught carving anyone else's name will be expelled.'

After prayers at nine o'clock all the boys were confined to their rooms, to work, to dream, or just to grow older quietly, except for the members of the Library, who were entitled to an additional half-hour of freedom in the Library, that shabby, spacious room presided over by a monstrous King Log of a radiogram in pinkish wood and decorated with an assortment of semi-nudes, culled from brave magazines a bit self-consciously and stuck up behind the darts' board to be riddled in moments of strain and frustration as full of holes as a makeshift constitution.

This was the time in which all their private business was enacted; misdemeanours punished, an irrational, godlike justice meted out, from time to time, elections held. This particular evening they elected Berwick to the Library. In accordance with time-honoured custom (time is always a good scapegoat at a Public School) the ceremonial at the election was laid down. The choice was made; the electors, capering like harpies, went to pay a visit on their new choice while the house captain, too dignified for social calls of this nature, visited the housemaster to inform him of the election.

Berwick lay on his bed, sweating for the Secret Service agent and his girl, as the man-eating crab sidled up the beach. The girl lay pegged down, naked, on the sand. Berwick could see her in a misty, vague way and in a little while he might be able to feel her too. His crowded room oppressed him and bothered him and distracted him from his lonely imaginings. A room dedicated to the glorification of the recent past. Photographs of sports teams looked down on him, their dicky-bird smiles frozen into smug self-consciousness. Striped and quartered caps hung rakishly from nails and leaving photographs of *eminents grises* ('Tony', 'Best wishes, Arthur', with dates) condescended from the mantelpiece. He read on in mounting excitement; he was too excited to do anything but read on.

When the Library pounded on the door, and swept in to shake him by the hand and duck him in the washbasin and scribble on his walls, and take his trousers off him and fling his things about him and generally impose themselves upon him, he was a second or two summing up the situation (he had to obliterate the crabs from his mind) and then he looked modestly about him and said:

'Well, that was a surprise.' Which was fine. He had kept up the game of make-believe just as they knew he would. You could always rely on Berwick to respect the conventions; God bless him.

Phillips lay snugly in the hollow of his sheets, secure in the warmth, in the darkness, unhatched, considering Scarfe and his strange faith. It had not been necessary to seek out Scarfe after all, which was just as well because he had thus been able to play the householder to Scarfe's newspaperboy. Because householders don't go calling on newspaperboys any more than mountains do Mahomets. Scarfe had come himself, nervously, as a Mahomet has every right to be, with a deprecating rat-tat-tat with the second knuckle of the forefinger and his little brown eyes a-twinkle – if not afire – with the admiration – if not the love – of God, and his little round head nodding like a bladder on a stick to emphasize his points, and his plaintive East-Anglian voice throbbing with emotion, almost with ecstacy. And it was the very poor-fishiness of the apparition that had moved Phillips in this queer way.

It was nice, too, not to be newspaper-boyish for a change. Sick as Phillips was with Morgan and Pemberton and their ways, he had been brusque with Scarfe for a start. As he always was. As everyone always was. A kind of Christmas-box brusqueness.

'Well, what is it?'

Scarfe had stayed quiet, smiling like a spastic, Phillips thought. He had seen a documentary on television in which . . .

'Do a brace, spill the beans.'

Scarfe moistened his lips:

'May I sit down, Tom?'

'Tom?' Nobody ever called him that. What was Scarfe doing calling him that? How did Scarfe know he was called that?

'Yes, yes, I suppose so.'

'Have you been confirmed, Tom?' Again? Tom again? What was this, a hunt ball? 'You haven't, have you, Tom?'

'No.'

'Why not?'

'Didn't feel like it, I suppose.'

'But you are C. of E.? I mean, you go to communion?'

'No. Not really.'

'Do you know what you're missing? You do, don't you, Tom? You *do* know?'

Phillips laughed. 'What is all this, anyway?' And at this point to his, Phillips's, surprise, Scarfe had launched really eloquently, considering the East-Anglian and all that, into an evangelistic plea for his, Phillips's, help in bringing The Faith to the unfortunate and misguided, well not exactly heathen, but . . . Phillips was naturally incredulous, dumbfounded, that, of all people, Scarfe, of all self-effacing people, would have had the nerve, would have had the face to launch out into all this Elmer Gantry stuff. He was – well, he was almost moved by it.

'You see,' Scarfe had besought, his narrow forehead glistening with sincere sweat and a black bogy dangling from his nose, 'there's so much we could do, you and I together. I'm not much of a one for impressing people, I know that, but with you, Tom, to set the example and to *talk* to them (they'd listen to you, even Morgan would listen to you) and me to take them on from there, and the Bishop finally to take them in – have you met the Bishop, Tom? We could do so much together. I mean, it's not as though we'd be alone in it, because—'

But it appeared that Fate thought otherwise, because at that moment the supper gong had gone, and Scarfe's eloquence, which had rather run its course anyway, was stifled by something far more everyday; macaroni cheese. Scarfe liked macaroni cheese and he had worked up an appetite.

But looking back on it from the warmth and snugness of his hollow-in-the-sheets (they had been clean that morning, and cold when he first got in, but now!) Phillips was struck by the ugly East-Anglian's sincerity, eloquence, and, yes, courage, heaven knows; in short he was struck by his faith, and envied it, and would like to, and very possibly might (or so it seemed in his sheets) come in with him on it. After all it was nothing to be ashamed of, though Morgan and Pemberton, no doubt, would laugh themselves silly if they should get to hear about their young protégé, their young Keats with the literary aspirations, being taken in by an East-Anglian shit-shoveller, which was what they called him among themselves . . .

And off Phillips sailed into a dream about a bishop riding on the back of for some reason a windmill at a gymkhana; and, poor old bishop, he kept getting knocked off by the sails. And there was Manningham, with a fly-button undone, shouting: 'Ah, but if you carve *your* name . . . Ah, but if you carve *your* name . . .'

About this time, or a little later, the Bishop, a virgin bachelor wedded to the Church, who was being put up during his visit in the house of one of the chaplains, was straining his neck out of the window, looking round the angle of the gable, to where he could just see, through a lighted pane, the eldest daughter of his host, a rather doughy sort of girl who was awfully good on the 'cello, in the act of removing her waist petticoat.

CHAPTER TWO

MORGAN generally spent his holidays with Pemberton at Crawley Hall. There were probably two reasons for this. One of them was that Morgan's parents had divorced and become even more difficult to live with singly than together. Sir Theobald Morgan of Towneley Hall had always been a vain man with the secure vanity of a title, an estate, and a deceitful smile, and it was for vanity that he had married Camilla Coppings, without doubt the most beautiful and presentable débutante of her year, a memorable year for débutantes. Sir Theobald Morgan remembered it well. Camilla had played upon his weakness, which grew to such proportions that for him to enter a hotel lobby (even a public bar, provided that it was public enough) with his lovely young girl-friend, fiancée, bride, on his arm, was an almost sensual delight. She was a sweet girl as well as a beauty, everybody said, there being nothing much else positive to be said about her – at least *behind* her back, and, if she was not accomplished, well, after all, it was not really she who had to do the accomplishing any more. So that it was doubly depressing and boring for him when he slammed the door of his Lagonda shut on her hand (they were even yet on their honeymoon!) and Camilla had to have the four fingers amputated. Of her introductory or shaking hand. In Sicily. It wasn't much of an accident when you consider other accidents in the nineteen thirties, but it was quite enough to remove the gilt from a rather gingery marriage. And although Camilla took it pretty hardly, weeping saltily over her inlaid manicure set, it was Sir Theobald who minded most, now that just about the only place he could take her

- to mix socially, you understand – was hotel lobbies and
such, and then only with her hands in a muff. And what
was the point of a beautiful wife, if she was only on show in
the winter months in hotel lobbies and such? When moreover she could only nod a greeting or click heels like one of
those totally unfeminine fascists. Oh, he had every reason
to lock her in the Towneley Hall library for long periods
at a time, not that she was an especially keen reader, and
so she had every reason after twenty or so bibliophobic
years, to demand a divorce. And Sir Theobald found himself another beauty with long, tapering fingers, and she
launched herself in a big way, and Morgan spent the
holidays at Crawley Hall with Pemberton, though, as I
said, he probably had another reason for this.

Pemberton's parents had the full complement of fingers
on the other hand, and were not divorced. They did not
have enough imagination. They lived instead in a kind of
limbo in which pretence passed for sentiment, sentiment
for emotion, and emotion for any exigencies unprovided
for. They had, besides their son, an unexceptional
daughter, Joanna, who was being launched for her
maiden voyage through the uncharted and unexplored
seas of London society, totally unseaworthy and dreadfully
ill-prepared for those marauders lying in wait to fire across
her bows, hole her, despoil her, and leave her as a ghost-
ship adrift in the regions of ice and snow. That is, if they
could be bothered with her at all, which was dubious.
H.M.S. Joanna, who could have been such a popular
little paddle-steamer, all beer and barnacles.

Sir Charles Pemberton was a short, rubicund chap, pink
and white as a puppy's belly, who was by no means as
jolly as he looked. That colour in his cheeks could have
been the after-glow of port . . . he never touched it; and
his expanding waist was not the residue of a life of
Epicurean banqueting – it was just his metabolism. He

ran to fat, as some men run to hounds, grimly, by inheritance not by choice. Yes, really he was miserable in spite of his one perverse delight in reading from St. Paul's less hilarious epistles to a bucolic and bovine congregation in the local church. And the weekdays he had long since found to be for him without point and without amusement.

His two interests were his ancestors, who were a grey, uninteresting lot, however royally painted, and his collection of stamps. He was a man without a mission, and he was waiting to die. His wife had no intention of ever doing so and regarded death as no more than weakness or a lack of character in others – she was a blowsy, vivacious creature but 'county' too, and her life had been little more than a string of disappointing rendezvous. Finally, on one occasion towards the end of the war, she had formed a liaison with the Second Lieutenant in the Crawley branch of the Home Guard – Sir Charles being Commanding Officer – and, on a series of manœuvres whose purpose was to defend a nearby cosmetics factory from hordes of unmade-up, indeed invisible, Nazis, was discovered by her husband coupling with the officer behind some defensive earthworks. Having watched what had long been the comedy of the parish with his own eyes, or at least through his army binoculars, Sir Charles had informed his wife that enough was enough and that if ever she tried anything similar again he would slit her throat, and that to make assurance doubly sure he was ordering a double bed from the Times Furnishing Company and that the two of them would share it for the rest of their lives – or at least until the death of one of them. What could the cruelly treated Lady Alison do but submit? Since her husband had every intention of sleeping by but not with her and since she had no money of her own with which to buy a divorce, her position was parlous. Forcibly

repressed, she had had to take refuge since the war in
nervous attacks to which Sir Charles, a reasonable man at
heart, was prepared to submit. A little percussion after so
many horns . . .

So that Morgan and Pemberton had little enough
reason to have been very much bettered by their elders
and betters, which was the principal cause of their looking askance at the world with an irony beyond their
years.

The Easter holidays lasted four weeks and the two of
them spent them in the languid luxury of boredom, a
boredom only relieved by aping the idiosyncrasies of the
noble and notable guests who drove down in Bentleys for
long week-ends which they spent in a seasonal and dis-
criminate slaughter of any fish, flesh and fowl who were
foolish enough to have concluded their mating. The noble
and notable guests themselves, who however had not yet
concluded *their* mating, were immune from such a very
peremptory and utilitarian kind of fate. And, if it were not
for Lady Alison's terrible nervous migraines, on which
occasions Crawley Hall was best avoided, Sir Charles and
his wife would have been regarded as the perfect host and
hostess by their guests. Some of these guests brought their
daughters with them and Morgan and Pemberton on a few
occasions roused themselves from their lethargy, put down
their whiskies and their billiard cues, and endeavoured to
plumb the depths of the débutante mind. But they soon
retired from the field, stunned into silence by the pusil-
lanimity and gaucherie and pinheadedness (not to put too
fine a point on it) of these green girls; girls whose deepest
feelings were reserved for their powerful and long-
suffering fathers and horses, neither of whom (alas!) would
they ever be able to marry. Yet there was one girl who so
far exceeded the rest in mawkishness and witlessness that
the boys were quite roused to incredulity and determined

to discover what were the clockwork mechanics of such a parody. The way it happened there was nearly a nasty accident.

Pemberton said casually after dinner one Saturday:

'We're thinking of going off to the Crawley fair this evening. Would you like to join us, Clarissa?' Sir Charles and Lady Alison exchanged raised eyebrows over the Bombe Pompadour (a pretty picture!) but Clarissa showed her Wimpole Street teeth.

'Oh, how absolutely blissy!' she shrilled, 'Oh, how divine!'

'God's in the dodgems, all's right with the world,' muttered Morgan.

'I say, Mumsie, we're off to the fair. Isn't it a kill? Terribly kind of you to ask me and all that. Actually.'

'Oh, but that's absolutely all right,' said Pemberton, 'actually. Our pleasure.'

And off the three of them went.

Pemberton, who was already seventeen, drove them in his open red M.G. He drove fast and bitterly, the shimmering radiator swallowing up the cats' eyes, the belching exhaust spewing them out. Startled rabbits and field-mice balanced mesmerized on the tarmac, or broke the spell and scuttled for the ditches. It was rather cold for the time of year.

'It's rather cold for the time of year. Actually,' said Clarissa. The waves of her hair were breaking in the wind. No one answered her, but it may have been because they couldn't hear her. You never knew with Morgan. He was sitting between them on the back of the seats like a parson blessing a bride and bridegroom. But she would not make a pretty bride, Clarissa; nobody thought so. Not even her aunts who shook their heads and discussed her heredity. Nor was she fascinating. Nor musical. Nor gamine. Nor deep. Especially not deep. She had short arms and legs, thick ankles and wrists, and big ears. Between these extremities she was ordinary enough, but above the ears there was nothing considerable at all. She would have done well enough in a factory behind a paint-sprayer or a comptometer, but the unfortunate girl was doomed to a position in life which demanded from her those qualities with which she was the least endowed. And the terrible thing is that she never knew how unhappy she was. She was content . . .

On their arrival at the fairground Pemberton bought them each hot dogs, complete with mustard, onion and pickle. Clarissa laughed a great deal and insisted that she would be sick, then took a dainty mouthful, squealed, fanned her face with her hands and eventually brought out with extraordinary emphasis:

'Oh, it's absolutely divine!'

'Hot gods,' muttered Morgan, then took her hand and led her, protesting, to the Big Dipper.

'Oh, look, the Big Dipper,' cried Clarissa.

Pemberton bought the tickets ('Three, actually') and they shared the front car between them. As they began the slow climb up to the summit of the run and slowly, inevitably, made their way under the notice-board ('Please keep your seats and your hands inside the car') to the point of no return when things begin to gather speed and lose control, Clarissa became absolutely frightened.

'Oh, oh!' she cried, 'I'm absolutely frightened.'

Pemberton stood up.

'But it's all terribly good fun. And frightfully, frightfully English. But here we go!' People shouted to him to sit down, but he remained standing all the way round, his thighs pressed against the safety bar.

'Whoosh!' Clarissa kept saying as soon as she got over her initial terror. Almost unconsciously she kept pulling the skirt of her dress down over her knees. 'Whoosh! Whoosh!'

After the Big Dipper they shot ping-pong balls out of fountains and saw what the butler saw, which was nothing to what the butler saw in Crawley Hall, and rolled pennies, and stared at the Wasp-woman.

'Do you sting?'

'Oh, yes, dearie, definitely. Try touching me.' But Clarissa was frightened again: 'I wouldn't want to be a Wasp-woman' and Pemberton agreed that it would not be much of a career for a girl of her talents.

'No Union,' added the Wasp-woman surprisingly. And they took a turn on the roundabouts – devils on horseback – and then Morgan began to clink the money in his pocket and whistle and look at the stars until Pemberton recognized the signal. Pemberton said:

'When you've quite finished star-gazing,' and Clarissa said:

'Oh, look, there's the Plough, and that must be the Pole Star, then, and what's that one?' And Pemberton said:

'Orion's jock-strap,' but Morgan was not amused, and Clarissa – surely she couldn't have heard? – went serenely on, 'Oh, is it? Then I suppose that must be his face there and that his sword and—' A heavy bank of clouds blowing in from the West Midlands modestly covered the rest of Orion. They moved on until Pemberton pointed:

'The ghost train.'

'Why not? Why not?'

'A million shrieks, a million thrills.'

'Ah, go on.'

'Ooh, do let's; I've never been on one, and they don't have them on the Continent, and it will be absolute heaven.'

'Roll on the gospel train,' said Morgan.

The bored young man who dissected their tickets – a

kind of modern-day Charon – showed no reaction to Clarissa's gasped: 'Oh, gosh, will I hate it?' No visible reaction, but it may be that he had a reply ready that was burning him up within. They sat in their little compartment, and were grudgingly shoved through the *porte cochère* which took them 'to the other side of the grave'.

A skeleton sat up and gaped sheepishly at them. Clarissa screamed. A bat fluttered just overhead. Clarissa screamed and put her hands to her hair. Something wet hit them in the face. Clarissa screamed and Pemberton caught his breath. It was just then that Morgan put his hand under Clarissa's skirt and took silk, so to speak. Pemberton was in on it too. Clarissa screamed and leapt up in her seat just as an old man with a torn lantern and gyves came quavering out of the darkness at her. The two of them met in a kind of *impasse*, while the little car clattered bravely on through the other *porte cochère* and into the physical world again. On the way through the doors Clarissa, now slumped over the windscreen of the vehicle in what could have been an hysterical fit, caught her head on a metal support and was knocked unconscious. Embracing her, and looking absurdly shabby in the red glare of the 'Rockets to the Moon', was the cardboard cut-out model of the old man with the lantern.

They had to pay the bored young man quite a lot to repair the damage and to ask no questions, although it is true that for half an hour after the disturbance he did bigger business with the ghost train, even without the old man, than he had done since the onset of his boredom. Clarissa soon recovered and some brandy from the glove-compartment of the car brought the colour back into her cheeks. But she didn't talk much on the way back and Morgan and Pemberton were quietly content – in the true scientific tradition – with their sociological survey.

Scarfe's father ran a small general farm in East Anglia. At least in the old days it had been small, the old days when in the spring Scarfe had happily assisted in the lambing, foaling and calving, though for the most part the animals could be relied upon to get on with that themselves; he had been content to busy himself hedging and ditching, propping up the branches of the old, gnarled, Victoria plum trees in full blossom, pitching and creosoting, whitewashing and manuring, and meditating. He had been very content. For there is a heart-warming friendliness in the spring landscape of East Anglia, where the white cumulus clouds hang like cherubim over the green copses, and their bums turn pink in the evening sun. But all that was in the old days. Oh, last April the cherubim had still hung there, but in the shadows of their bellies as they sailed across the sky changes had been taking place. His father had greeted him proudly, but had not been at the station to meet him. He had been too busy. He talked then of 'expansion', also of 'specialization'. These were new words for him, new ideas, and the newest of all was 'battery system'. 'Progress' was important and 'catering to the tastes of the machine age' was too, and it all broiled down to this. Geoffrey Scarfe had installed, as other more radical farmers had done some time ago, a broiler plant for 5,000 chicks.

Geoffrey Scarfe was a weak man, easily swayed and impressed by big words, big money or the latest big fashion, yet with the inbred subtlety and cynicism that all farmers seem to share. He was moderately pious himself, at least in observance, and a believer, but did not regard his Maker as a friend; too often he had prayed for rain to be rewarded by a drought, or, worse still, a hail-storm that had flattened his crops in an hour. Things had been made deliberately difficult for Adam, and, through him, for all farmers, and Geoffrey Scarfe was by nature inclined to blame in equal proportions, Woman, who had tempted him, and God, who had let her. He was not a rich man, but, by cynicism – leaving as little as possible to malignant chance – and by hard work, he had been enabled to save enough to install this plant. Young Scarfe had not at first dared to remonstrate with his father, but, when he visited the plant, he had been sickened. The five thousand chicks, White Wyandottes with their rosy combs and yellow skins, Rhode Island Reds, glowing rich and dark, lived in a corrugated iron shed, on a square foot of sawdust per bird. They were heavily drugged to keep them alive, and, to counteract the very real danger that they might tear each other to pieces from hunger and boredom, they had been debeaked. For their life-span of three months, they were kept in near-darkness under a dim red light. Adjoining the broiler plant was a deep pit into which the poorer specimens were thrown to make room for others. As his father showed him round, young Scarfe's gum-boots had squashed a couple of chicks (there was not much room for visitors, which was just as well), but he had been told not to worry: 'I can afford to lose a few,' he had added, 'do you know how much I save by this method in one year?' He had then told his son that he hoped he would take his turn as slaughterman. Scarfe had tried it once, but the sight of the birds, strung by their feet to a moving rail as they came to him to have their throats cut – they took two minutes to reach him – turned his stomach so quickly that he was forced to return to his whitewash bucket and his creosote pail.

He had one night asked his father timidly:

'Is it necessary? I mean, the way you keep them like that?' and his father had laughed and replied: 'Son, it pays; look at the figures.' He had then talked of 'pound of feed per pound weight of gain in body' and 'minimum of fifty per cent production'.

But all that had taken place last year, and this spring there was another surprise awaiting him at home.

'How're things, dad?'

'Pretty good, Gentleman,' his father frequently called him that when he was cheerful, 'do you know anything about the Dutch veal system?'

No. Scarfe knew nothing about it. His father soon explained to him that the methods of farming broiler chicks had been recently extended to include other animals and so much success had attended his first venture that he had been encouraged (and enabled) to try his luck with the broiler house for veal. His father took him round.

A barn had been converted and slatted floors a few inches off the ground had been added. Specially selected calves were tethered in small pens with their heads in wooden stocks.

'The point is,' his father explained, 'to produce milk-white veal cheaply. I save sixpence a pound this way. Iron. Now that's the danger. If they are allowed iron in any edible form, their flesh becomes discoloured. As you see, they have no straw. Straw contains iron. Now, Gentleman, do you know why they have these stocks around their necks?'

No. The gentleman had no idea. But he looked at his father in amazement. This was a money-mad stranger.

'Well, it's like this. The beasts get so mad for iron, they try to lick the urine off the floor. Well, we can't have that, can we? When we slaughter these at three months' old, their flesh will be as white as your mother's milk . . .'

Scarfe had gone to bed early that night, the first of the holidays. Holidays! When he remembered those calves the word seemed bitter to him. Next morning he had asked his father if he needed the extra money. The reply had been:

'Well, if we're to keep you in the manner to which you're accustomed.' So it was *his* responsibility.

'But is it natural, Father, to keep them like that?'

'Is it natural to keep you like that?'

Scarfe was a 'guinea-pig'. That is to say, he was one of those boys unfortunate enough to have been selected from a grammar school (in Diss) to go on to Eton. Guinea-pigs were chosen on all-round ability; Scarfe was chosen as a talented mathematician, a sound, reliable half-back and an unfailing church-goer; his mother had been so proud of him, and his father in the way he might have prided himself on a prize bull, and he had been so proud too, and pleased because they were . . . But at Eton they hardly played soccer at all, and when everyone else attended chapel daily by compulsion, he had not much merit in that. As for his mathematics, his first Algebra lesson had been a fiasco. *A*, *b*, and *c*, those friends he loved and understood, had been horribly transmogrified into *a*lligators, *b*ison, and *c*rocodiles, and then five minutes later, even more horribly, into *a*ttlees, *b*evans, and *c*hurchills. He understood them no longer. On the other hand without being melodramatic about it he had learnt how to suffer all right. 'How can a guinea-pig show he's pleased when he hasn't got a tail to wag?' And poor Scarfe couldn't show he was pleased because he wasn't, and couldn't wag his tail like the others as they swung to and fro on their family trees.

Scarfe determined to do something about his East-Anglian squeak; and he determined to do something about his father's 'new methods'. So every day in the fields as he splashed away at the outhouses (happily while the love of God and the Bishop almost burst his ribs) he practised his diction, and every evening before great bowls of stew and soup, he practised his eloquence. And something strange happened. His father seemed to grow afraid of him. He used the word 'Gentleman' more and more often and more and more ironically. He didn't take him with him to the pub for darts any more. And, strangest of all, he began to defer to his son's opinion.

'But don't you see, I mean, that morally you have no right to treat the animals this way?'

'Well, yes, Gentleman, I was saying to your mother the other day about this—'

'I mean, I don't want the money, and I won't take the money, if that's how it came.'

Doubtfully: 'Well, it's not only the money, son . . .'

'Please, Father, don't put any more calves in the broiler-house.'

'I'll see, Gentleman, I'll see . . .'

And he took care that, at any rate, while his son was home, he did not add any calves to the others. The fun was out of it . . .

And Scarfe felt gratified, and sometimes even happy, but when he went to bed, he counted the days, he counted the days, he counted the days.

Phillips, who was an only child, and his parents, who were only parents, took a ten days' holiday on the Thames in their motor-launch, the *Queen of the Andes*. They started at Putney and within five days had reached Lechlade. Retrospectively, Phillips remembered little of the journey upstream; he was struck if anything with a sense of cheapness, of vulgarity, where he should have been most elevated. At Hampton Court, Bisham Abbey and Windsor Castle, instead of being inspirited by the stories of Henry VIII and Anne of Cleves or sobered by the thought of the old, black Queen Victoria mourning dearest Albert defiantly in front of her journal, he was appalled at the vulgarity of the soulless, sluggish tourists with their beastly, sticky children, and, at Bisham, affronted by the hearty camaraderie of the young gods and goddesses doing eurhythmics on the lawn.

But he nodded his approval on the matutinal glowing spires and gasworks of Oxford and marvelled at the perdurable sweep of the valley, sinister and overwhelming at My Lady Ferry, Cliveden, where the water-snakes swum from treed bank to treed bank and might as well be crocodiles, and friendly and open at Wallingford, once scourged by the Black Death, where now the cows stand exquisitely jig-sawed as they graze in their own sun-and-shade. And he wandered contentedly through the small riverside towns, Marlow, Henley, Wargrave, with their foaming weirs and their fairgrounds and their flags and their Swiss pâtisseries. Yet none of this, not even this, impressed him, or was memorable to him, half as much as the girl he met in Shiplake Lock.

It was late afternoon, and the shadows of the high sculpted banks cast their substance across the river. In the lock itself the bollards and the sluices stood out in sharp contour against the diffused sunlight and her yellow frock over its stiff petticoats billowed like a bright mid-afternoon sail. What was left of the fading light seemed almost to exhale from her as if she were the source of all energy; she moved as if she were too. Had she had a parasol as a halo about her curls she might have stepped straight out of the frame of an impressionist painting. He was so dazzled by her (yes, almost literally dazzled) that he forgot his boathook and let the *Queen of the Andes* ride up sharply against her boat before coming to his senses.

'Watch it!' she called in an unsympathetic voice, running over to fend him off. More than a glow-worm, more than a fire-fly.

'Sorry.'

'No need to be. No harm done.' Her boat lay higher in the water than theirs, and consequently he had to look up at her slightly. The sun was setting behind her, ringing her outline with flames. Like an eclipse. That made her the

moon presumably; therefore chaste. He had to shade his
eyes. It was a little boy attitude in some way. He could
have been staring out to sea and the Spanish Armada.

'Really not?'

'Uh-uh. No thanks to you.'

Sublunary Phillips was at his most chivalrous then. As if
he really had sat beside Sir Walter Raleigh. He was not
exactly scared of girls, nor suspicious of them; a little of
fear, a little of suspicion made up his attitude towards the
unknown quantity.

In any case he must show respect; that must be right. A
respectful man and a respectable girl; yes, but it was
difficult to see how a couple like that would ever get on
speaking terms. And speak to her he must. So far he had
not shown himself to be any different from all the other
river-going (and, blast them, maybe not so respectful)
young men. If he didn't say something funny or memorable soon she would surely have lost interest in him. He
couldn't think what to say, not for the life of him. Then to
his surprise:

'Going on far?' she called.

'I don't know. It's not up to me. The locks close soon.'

'At sundown is it?'

'I think so.' He knew very well that it was, but had no
desire to appear a know-all. 'And you?'

But she was busy now, hanging on to the slimy chain
hand over hand to keep her end of the boat from straying
too far into the middle as the water churned out. They
sank down together, as fast as toy boats in a bath, so that
the sun was at once cut off and she became only a pale
reflection of her former self, a moon of the moon (but very
charming), and all the walls were green and damp and
dripping. She slapped herself vigorously until the yellow
dress swayed from her waist like a pendulum.

'Damn those mosquitoes!' But she sounded quite friendly

towards the mosquitoes, as friendly as towards him even.

'Haven't you got any stuff for them?' That was daring of him, and he hoped she wouldn't consider it too forward. Already he was aware of his father and mother looking on curiously. Their faces as usual to him seemed enigmatic. Neither approving nor disapproving. No help at all. Hers had not put in an appearance and must have been below. Poor yellow orphan! He was also suddenly aware of his knees.

'Only soap.' Well, that was an odd thing to say; what did she do to the mosquitoes with soap? Throw it at them?

'Why, what do you do with soap? Throw it at them?'

She laughed absolutely unaffectedly. He didn't think he had ever heard anyone laugh as naturally as that. He must have impressed her to make her laugh like that. He simply must. And then, out of the blue:

'Well, good-bye. Watch your boathook!'

For the heavy lock gates had dragged silently open and her boat, sliding swiftly from its moorings, chugged into the main stream. *Genevra*. That was its name (not hers) but he would remember her by that. Things must have names; memories especially, he decided. And there was always a chance he might see her again.

Running unusually fast Phillips made for the wheel-house and asked his father to let him take over the controls. His father, mouth amiably twisted by sucking at a pipe – he fancied himself as a sea-dog, but didn't quite like to chew quids of tobacco – hesitated, deliberated (as he did before every decision from something as trivial – trivial? – as this to the taking over of a chain of confectioners') and agreed (as he generally did with the take-overs). He was a man of – malleable – iron.

Nearing Wargrave – they were on their return journey – Phillips caught a glimpse in a backwater of a sparkle of yellow and wrenched at the wheel. His mother, repressing a malediction as soup from the saucepan spattered the gas-ring, tightened her lips. But Phillips had an appetite for more than soup. The yellow dress had preceded him like his own private pillar of fire and they were to spend the night as neighbours. For there, moored already, her elegant stern rising in a graceful parabola from the water like any water-nymph, posed *Genevra*.

'Can we moor here?' he shouted to his father and threw the painter on to the bank.

The boat was the same one but there was a stranger on it. A tall young man, bare to the waist, sophisticatedly slim, was emptying a bucket over the side. Even performing so simple a job, it was clear to Phillips that this was the King of Slops, the absolute Baron of Buckets; it was a shock to him. His river-nymph had been boarded already. How stupid of him. Of course he should have known. He should have guessed. It was inevitable, as inevitable as that the moon should wane. He jumped ashore and busied himself with securing the painter, keeping his back to the boats. Sweet reliable Mother Earth. He would like to have plastered his face with mud, taken the boathook in his hand, poising it like an assegai, and turned on that slim young man with a horrible war-cry curdling in his throat. And then from behind every tree others like himself, black as sin, would leap on board that elegant vessel, tie the young white man to the mast-head, had there been a mast-head, and – do something unpleasant to him, while he, James Arthur Phillips, seized the maiden in his ruffianly arms, and . . .

He wished they could move on again, moor elsewhere, but his father would never stand for that. If there was one quality his father wished to instill in his son, it was resolution. 'It's all right for women to change their minds, my son,' he would say, 'we admire them in spite of it, but you, sir, must be manly, must be resolute. Take your time, but keep your word. People will respect you for it.' And then he would quote some words of Doctor Johnson's or Lord Chesterfield's, complacent in the authority vested in him by these great men. Admiring them for their breadth of vision, he could somehow always find in them justification for his own narrow nature and intolerance. Furthermore, he was triumphantly unaware of the paradox. Phillips looked up to him, loved him naturally, and was very much afraid of him. For a little while longer.

No, he'd just have to stick it, close up to her all night and as far away as Timbuctoo, while that young god dispossessed him. Trying not to look back at the *Genevra*, he jumped on to the *Queen of the Andes* and into the galley. His mother, a vague sort of cluster of a woman who used to cry sometimes for her lost youth into the soup and for other things that they could only guess at, was stirring browning into the gravy. She was always cooking. Looking past her he could see his own reflection in the black glass of the port-hole. It was getting dark. The face looked back at him quizzically. It was a face that formed an upside-down triangle whose apex rested dangerously on a scraggy neck. From the small sharp-pointed chin, fluffy with the premature beginnings of a beard, up past the transparent semi-circular ears to a broad convex brow, the face was symmetrical and polite. It was an interested, not an interesting, face, unless you studied it closely. Strands of corn-coloured thatching hung loose over his blue eyes. Trying to see it as a stranger might see it, Phillips was not happy with his face. It was not very resolute. Still, he was stuck with it; no two ways about that. He was not double-faced. A voice at the port-hole. The voice of the moon surely:

'Could you let us have some sugar?'

'Who's that?' from his mother.

'Well I don't know. I'll go and see.' And he jumped ashore, to Timbuctoo in a stride.

'Thought it was you,' she said, 'recognized the boat.'

'Yes, it's me all right,' said Phillips, looking beyond her towards the tall, bare, active giant with muscles like little oysters and an emphatic fuzz of hair on his chest.

'Have you any sugar to spare? Did you follow us here?' She seemed to show about the same amount of interest in the two questions; there was no begging in the first, no malice in the second; there was nothing much in either.

Just about this time when sugar and hunting were more or less hanging over them in the air like mistletoe at a Christmas party, the giant stepped out of his trousers and leapt over the side of the boat in a long rakish curve. The gnats darted away over the shining river and the whole length of his body entered the water with as little trouble as a hypodermic needle piercing the skin. When eventually he reappeared – and any *human* lungs must have burst in half the time – he shot waist-high out of the river, shaking a tiara of water out of his hair. The girl didn't bother to look round. She even takes him for granted, thought Phillips, despising himself more and more.

'That's my brother,' said the girl, with an airy, off-hand gesture, 'perhaps you'd like to come swimming with me later?'

Phillips's mother and father and Jill's brother (it was Jill and he had had to rechristen his memories) had gone to bed presumably. It was growing cold now and the mist that rose from the river was the only witness to the heat of the day gone by. The slapping of the water against the bottom of the boats – that most nostalgic of all sounds – was intensified in the silence of the night; the rare, tenuous, moonshiny silence of that part of the night when even the night birds are scared into silence. There was still a translucency in the river and a star or two shone through the curved cyclorama of the sky. They had both slipped into sweaters after their bathe but their bare legs stretched out in front of them luminously like four big worms as they lay side by side on the bank. They hadn't touched each other yet except once by accident when Jill's hand had flapped against his as they raced towards the water.

Jill's abrupt manner that had so charmed Phillips earlier in the day, though not at all in keeping with the yellow dress, had mellowed now. It was a perfectly natural mellowing in the circumstances. Her voice had become soft and rather husky. And where Phillips had been charmed before, he was now enchanted and amazed.

'Feel like an intruder,' said Jill.

'Why?'

'The river has been here for so long, and what right have we to come churning it up with our propellers?'

'You know I was thinking just the same, 'cept about history. All the famous people who must have looked at the river much as we do like, you know, Henry the Eighth, and thought about it as we do, and now all the hateful trippers who sort of cheapen it all with their wirelesses and—'

'The river doesn't care though,' said Jill.

Phillips took a deep breath, and counted to seventeen.

'Gosh, you're pretty!' he said.

'Probably always were trippers anyway, I suppose . . . do you really think so?' She turned and looked at him questioningly, challenging him to repeat it.

'Yes, I've never seen anyone so pretty.' Then, suddenly daring, but impelled too by the warm proximity of the pretty girl who was pleased he had said she was pretty, he put out a hand, and traced the line of her eyebrow, rubbing it softly against the grain. His hand therefore was across her forehead. She shivered a little.

'Cold,' she said, 'must go to bed. Why are you doing that?'

He wanted desperately to express something in himself of an old problem, but could only find the clumsiest words. He couldn't expect that she would understand.

'Are you really with me in this?'

'Well, what do you think?'

'I wondered if there was really someone lying there within you, inside that body, behind those eyes.' He could tell by the ironical look on her face, flattered but ironical, like a woman who has unexpectedly been given an expensive present, that he should never have brought up the subject, that he had botched it already. He had to go on with it though now.

'I mean, are you actually there looking at me, thinking about what I'm saying . . . have you got a soul, Jill?' Now she laughed flirtatiously. She had dealt with that question. It had been an unfair one anyway, not within her terms of reference.

Phillips dug his toes into the grass. It was no good. The chance was past, gone, a memory without a name, this one, that he would be content to lose. He really might have reached her, but now there was nothing to it. He leaned over and kissed her eyebrow and then her lips, fairly tenderly, but not as he might have kissed if only she could have understood. She responded, and was shivering again now, spasmodically. It really was getting rather cold. It was the first time he had kissed a girl ever – outside the family – and he did it instinctively, but when she opened her mouth to his, he drew back instinctively.

'What's wrong?' she whispered.

'You're cold.'

'Yes.' He kissed her again, this time determined not to give himself away, and inserted a hand under her sweater, up to her left breast. Her bathing costume was still damp and he could feel her heart-beat, faint and fast. Her hair was wet, and smelt – strange – of the sea. She was still shivering. They got up, and she put a hand to the back of his neck.

'I must go to bed.' She kissed him quickly on the cheek and ran off without looking back. Tucking away his profound disappointment in some secure part of him, Phillips felt both pleased with himself and ashamed. 'Already?' he said aloud. 'So soon?'

In the morning, before 'striking camp' and moving on, Jill and he exchanged addresses, mumbled a little and didn't know what to say at all, but agreed, more or less, to see each other again before long. It was a cold, grey morning anyway and Jill was coughing like a carpentry shop.

'Which one do you mean, darling?' said the Honourable Mrs. Alethea Berwick to her son, 'the third from the left perhaps, my pet?'

'Mother, please.'

'But she has thighs like something in a butcher's shop, my lamb, and varicose veins.'

'Ssh, Mother, everyone's turning round.'

'Might I suggest, my angel, the one in the torn fish-net? The most successful of her high kicks are absolutely *transcendental*. Don't you admire her high kicks, my love?'

A tired businessman with a compromising face and a little damp moustache turned round and tried to look angry and authoritative. He succeeded only in looking beseeching, or possibly constipated.

'Ears, wrists and ankles,' continued Alethea, 'are such stuff as dreams are made on, ears in particular. Always check the ear-lobes, my dove, because ear-lobes are the signs of true breeding. Oh, but little torn fish-net is *beguiling*!'

'Please!'

'But the pleasure is mine if it gives you pleasure, my own. I shall go straight round afterwards and accost her. She is a lucky girl.'

'Mother!' Because the whole row in front had begun to tremble like a geyser about to gush.

'There's my little idol!' gushed Alethea, smoothing down the blond waves of his hair, and thinking how like his dear father he was becoming, the old crook.

Berwick slouched in silence till the end of the chorus, staring despondently at the chorus-girl with the beguiling ears. When the tap-dancer, a bored young man with marionette legs and gravy-stains down the front of his silk-faced dinner-jacket, flounced on in front of the drop to drown the noise of the revolve, Berwick whispered to his mother:

'Please, not tonight. Please.' His voice was vibrant and desperate, but the answer was succinct and to the point. The Honourable Mrs. Alethea Berwick lowered her opera glasses and fingered the triple string of pearls round her stately, unlined neck. And in her throaty, Godalming accents, she said:

'Balls, darling!'

'Cheese!' The fish-netted chorus-girl whistled through her teeth, 'you get me here on some phoney excuse . . .'

'Mother does,' corrected Berwick, wincing with embarrassment.

'You feed me up like a ruddy Paschal offering, you pay me to be agreeable . . .'

'*Pay* you?' said Berwick. 'Mother *paid* you. I thought, I mean I imagined . . .' But what was the difference? Merely a matter of terminology.

'And then *you* pay me to trot off home like I was some kind of a witch.' No, not you, thought Berwick.

'What the hell is all this anyway, for crying out loud?'
Berwick wasn't crying out loud, but he wasn't far off it.
So that was what his mother was up to. He could understand her well enough hiring chorus-girls to teach him the
facts of life, that part of the whole hideous business made
perfectly good sense, but why in heaven's name didn't she
just tell him what he needed to know (like those blasted
positions, for instance) and be done with it. Surely she
couldn't be embarrassed. Not Lady Hormones, as London
called her, who used to delight in getting him to . . . He
shuddered at the childhood recollection.

Anyway, here he was, feeling like something squashed
on the road after all the pink champagne she'd pumped
into him, with a rather more than décolleté female chew-
ing him over from the corner of the counterpane. This, his
seventeenth birthday, was the first time his mother had
gone to these extremes, and there was nothing he could
think of to ensure that it would be the last. She must have
seen it all as a kind of birthday treat for him, the theatre,
the pink champagne, and this. Some birthday, some treat.
He didn't think he was going to enjoy manhood. The
chorus-girl moved sinuously over to him and slipped a
hand inside his shirt; her own remarkable costume had
fallen away still further to reveal, among other things,
that she had not removed her body make-up before
coming round. Everything about her was duplicity, well
almost everything . . . She pulled seductively at one end
of his bow-tie, and almost throttled him. So much for his
new knot. The room began to rise and fall, advance and
recede, under and before him. The comingled smells of
greasepaint and sweat were suffocating him.

'Look here,' he said desperately, thrusting his signet-
ring – just about all he had left on him – at her, 'I mustn't,
I can't, I shouldn't, don't you see, I'm in training.'

'Well, sugar, that's convenient isn't it?' she murmured

and clutched at him; to fulfil the terms of her contract. The signet-ring fell to the floor and rolled away under the dressing-table. It was a memento of his father – his only one. With his last reserves of energy (what was happening to him?) he slipped past her clutches into the bathroom, locked the door and sank, semi-conscious, on to the lavatory seat. From beyond the door he could hear clatterings and bangings like an army on the loot. That would be the girl rifling his drawers. He could hear her swearing passionately to herself:

'Cheese! What a way to spend Passion Week! Of all the crummy geeks . . .' and so on into the night. It wasn't much of a womb, huddled there for hour upon hour with a bath mat around his shoulders, but for the first time that evening a sense of security began to dispel the mists of alcohol that befuddled his brain. A big, warm, wet tear rolled on to the tip of his nose and hung there like a precious stone. Eventually he clawed his way to the medicine chest and with a pitiful sob grasped the bottle of Milk of Magnesia.

A poor mother substitute.

CHAPTER THREE

Mrs. Molarkey encouraged herself into the 'Ladies Only' compartment of a Southern electric train at Waterloo and infiltrated her niece, Hesta, after her. It was not strange that there should have been a 'Ladies Only' compartment on this particular train, seeing as how Mrs. Molarkey was on it too. For she was all lady through and through. For sheer bulk lady Mrs. Molarkey stood alone. A fine lady. A true-born lady. Her ladyship in full sail. However, her intense preoccupation with ladylikelihood had left her no time for being a woman and, to aid identification, she generally went around with her niece, who was a woman first and a lady only vicariously.

Mrs. Molarkey's trouble was that being a lady, even in the Welfare State, was not financially a very rewarding profession. As a woman she might have drawn family allowances, widows' benefits, orange-juice and milk, to say nothing of free pre-natal and post-natal care, with legal advice to help to squeeze out alimony if necessary; as a lady she drew nothing except admiring glances. Not always admiring either. Living nearer Notting Hill than Kensington, nearer Shepherd's Bush than Hammersmith, Mrs. Molarkey was not always received as a lady should be. In fact, when she went abroad (to the Portobello Market perhaps) she would find herself with an entourage of anything but respectful followers. They had taken recently to singing after her progress such jingles as:

> 'Mrs. Molarkey
> Married a darkey,

When she put the lights on
He was gone.'

which were total prefabrications and not even within the
realms of possibility. How should a lady react in such
circumstances? On one occasion she even lowered her
umbrella at her tormentors, but no, her breeding restrained her. Her meagre life-insurance pension (they
should have special terms for fat people anyway) had
recently, because of the rise in the cost of living, become
insufficient even for the Portobello Market, and Mrs.
Molarkey, from an obstinate instinct for self-preservation,
had found herself forced to advertise. It was not proper –
and she couldn't; it was not decorous – and she wouldn't;
it was not right – and she did. She advertised in the
properest of terms in the most decorous of journals, and it
must have been right (but it was bitter!) because, lo and
behold!, she was summoned to present herself at Manningham's house to be interviewed for the post of 'boys'
maid'. Domestic service! And her sixty years of propriety
uttered the syllables with scorn. Domestic service! And
her dewlap trembled as she thought of the pinching diet
enforced by those sixty years of propriety. She brought
along with her her niece for moral support, although she
was moral enough herself, and for material support,
although she had material enough herself, especially when
it came to pirouetting in and out of Southern electric
trains . . .

She was interviewed, if a passive tense can be applied
to as formidable and active a lady as Mrs. Molarkey, by
Manningham's 'Dame', or head-matron. This good lady,
who possessed a hereditary title, felt so very small, and
indeed looked so very small, in the presence of Mrs.
Molarkey, that she was almost physically afraid to turn
down her application, and engaged, not only Mrs.

Molarkey herself, but the niece too, in the capacity of secretary, a post which, though the niece might not fill it to perfection, Mrs. Molarkey could be relied upon to overflow into.

'Ai'm not accustomed to heavy domestic work,' Mrs. Molarkey had threatened in her resounding basso.

'But, Auntie . . .' the niece expostulated. She frequently expostulated and her aunt would sometimes talk severely to her about it, but poor Hesta was forced by this malignant thing inside her to continue to expostulate whenever the opportunity presented itself. She usually felt better afterwards.

The Dame had explained that Mrs. Molarkey's duties would include calling fifteen of the boys at seven in the morning, tidying their rooms and making their beds, and stewing tea for them in the afternoon. 'You will have a bed-sitting-room of your own opposite the Library, where I'm sure you'll quickly feel very much at home.'

'Ai'm not accustomed to making beds . . .'

'But, Auntie . . .'

'However, Ai realize that beds hev to be made, and Ai shall no doubt oblaige you bai demeaning maiself.'

'Well, thank you very much, Mrs. – em, yes, and I'm confident you will find the work very much to your liking.'

Mrs. Molarkey installed herself in her bed-sitting-room, or more picturesquely, wriggled into it like a snake with a new skin, attached the framed photograph of the Queen to the wall above the fireplace, and sat on her hams to await developments. The boys were not due back for the summer half for another couple of days, and she needed all that time to consider seriously what attitude it would be wise to adopt towards them. She had no experience of boys, at any rate of nice upper-crustaceous boys, but intuition signified to her that towards a real lady they would show only chivalry.

Oh no, not domestic service! It was more like lending the gentility a helping hand. Ah, it would be nice to be amongst her own people at last.

Once upon a time Mr. Manningham had arrived at Eton with the greatest possible zeal and the noblest intentions, a thin, young Cortes. He had just come down from the University, where he had had a most distinguished career, becoming Treasurer of the Union in his second year and hard-earning a first-class classical degree in his third. The choice had then lain between a job in the great, big, beautiful world of industry and the ascetic hermitage of a teaching career in a Public School. All night long, one, to tell the truth rather drunken, night he had wrestled with this problem, like Jacob with the angel, and had at length decided, after a truly mystical experience when he had observed his mortar-board spirit itself across the room towards him, to devote himself to self-sacrifice and the new generation. But the decision had relieved, rather than sanctified him, and he devoted himself to pedagogy (not quite hagiology), because he was not convinced that the rewards in industry were always honestly apportioned. Was it always the best and worthiest clerk who was summoned first to the director's office, or was it not rather the director's son, the director's nephew, the director's protégé? But at a Public School his distinctions would shine like platinum on a jeweller's tray, and maybe his relations, an undistinguished lot of modest wastrels, might one day even come to him for references. Furthermore, since he had been so successful at impressing undergraduates (he had figured weekly, in the nicest possible way, in the political scandal magazine), how much more ice would he cut with their younger brothers. Manningham liked to cut ice. And so he had smiled patronizingly when his friends had come skipping back from interviews with Unilever or I.C.I., as merry as children winning the musical chairs, and had laughingly advised them: 'Dog eat dog, you know. No more collections for the Canine Defence League from you.' But he didn't smile so brightly when he met them now, bringing their boys over in Bentleys. Not that he had done so badly himself. Superficially at any rate. After all, housemasters at Eton counted for something in the British hierarchy. But he wasn't married; he didn't drive a Bentley, and, what was worse, he didn't seem to impress anyone much any more. Where had he gone wrong?

His first half he had been a stern disciplinarian, working on the reasonable assumption that boys respect most what they fear most. But later on, when he wished to unbend a bit, get to know them a bit, understand and share their problems a bit, he found that they had put themselves (to some extent he had put them), beyond his reach. The reign of terror had worked only too well. He had invited his division to join him at the Lord's test match; they had opened their eyes wider and looked at each other ironically. He made all kinds of advances and was met with stony indifference, or, worse still, with downright suspicion. What was he after, they wondered? What was old Mockingbird's game? He had stated his terms, he had drawn up his own conditions, he must live by them.

And so, as the years passed, he withdrew into himself and gave up trying to please. His fierceness soured to weary sarcasm, a pose which boys like and trust the least of all, and no one ever suspected or made public any suspicions that Mockingbird Manningham was quite alone in the world, quite lonely, quite on his own; a terrible thing for anyone. Unmarried, and after fifteen years of frustration, he had inherited Hollingbourne House, a vicious red building something like a Post Office, clumsily constructed with all the misguided zeal of the mid-Victorians, which was a real pain in the neck whenever it was hot (or cold). Still, one doesn't judge oppidan houses at Eton by their elegance or by their modern amenities. College, where the seventy scholars live, is so overwhelmingly uncomfortable – scholars being by tradition ascetics – that oppidans, who pay for their discomfort, can have little justification for complaint on this score. The inheritance of Hollingbourne House was a just reward for implacability, and the assistant masters who concerned themselves with school politics (school whips you could call them but that would give the wrong idea) opined that Manningham was on the up-and-up. Manningham himself had a fervent hope that now at last he might have a chance, not any more to impress, but simply to gain the confidence, even the affection of one or two of his boys. Was it too much to ask?

The house he inherited had been in the hands of Philip Stratton, a botanist, a mountaineer, and, more eccentric by far, an optimist. For ten years he had been an impeccable housemaster by the simple process of hiding his eyes from the boys' excesses. 'There may be bullies in me house, I grant ye,' he said, 'but I've never seen 'em; there may be cheating, swearing, evil practices, and so on, but I've never heard of 'em. You see, I trust me boys, and they respect me trust. Nice boys, me boys, nice boys. So far as I know.' Consequently it came as something of a shock to 'Batty Stratty', after ten years to be informed by the Headmaster (to be informed, mind you) that a boy in his house, Carter Major, had been hiring out his younger brother, a particularly pretty child, to the rowing eight for three shillings a time. He had been incredulous. 'Me boys are nice boys.' 'No boys are nice boys,' the Headmaster had coldly replied, and, when Stratton had called Carter Major in to see him, he began to learn the wisdom of the Headmaster's words. Carter had implicated six others in

his house, all of whom had experienced in some measure
the brotherly love, and Stratton had been forced to expel
the two Carters; and it really did hurt him more than it
hurt them. The others, he obstinately maintained, had
been led astray, because 'most of me boys are nice boys'.
But the blow had killed the housemaster in Stratton, which
was almost all the invisible Stratton there was. He no
longer cared to attend the Field Game house matches and
cheer as he had been boisterously wont to: 'Fight 'em,
me boys! Fight 'em, me dear boys!' Instead he shut himself in his study and, surrounded by beautifully bound
volumes of Natural History, compiled his monumental
and comprehensive *Saga of the Matterhorn*, while waiting
for his sentence to expire. At fifty-eight Stratton had
become senile. The day-to-day running of the house had
fallen more and more on the freckled shoulders of the
sharp little Dame, who had truly relished this unlooked-
for access of power, and was therefore distressed to see
Manningham come striding into the house like a Viking
(except that physically he was too slim for the role). At
the time when Manningham took over, the feminine
influence had begun to make itself felt, and the house was
thoroughly demoralized, its prestige throughout the school
being at a very low ebb. If it had not been for Berwick and
a few other athletes, the house might have been thought
entirely obsolete.

This situation was all that Manningham could have
desired. Here was a challenge; a chance to prove himself,
above all to himself. He was glad that Stratton had failed.
He determined that he would be both tougher and more
understanding. Quickly reorganizing such things as
'Pupil Room', in which he superintended the boys' Latin
proses, and 'Privates', in which he watched over their
wider interests, he also recommenced the habit, disused by
Stratton, of visiting each boy in his own room every night,

when the boy was most dangerously alone. In this way he might come face to face with their problems, in which case they could hardly refuse his advice, or, if he didn't actually catch them at it, he could generally rely on the intimacy of the night-time to help worm out a few secrets. It was an arrangement more practical than romantic, but, by and large, it worked. The summer half just starting, his second half as housemaster, saw him well on the road, he thought, to success. The Headmaster was more guarded.

'The second half is the crucial one,' he said, 'they felt their way last half, this half they'll be feeling yours.' The Headmaster had quite a palate for epigram, and this had given him the unjustified reputation of cynicism. 'I'm not a cynic,' he would explain, 'just a sentimental old pessimist.'

At the end of the Easter half there was a considerable turn-over, Lansdowne and Marchant, two members of the Library (or prefects), leaving, and Defries entering his second term of office as Captain of the House. He had long been the cleverest boy in the house, had already been in Sixth Form for a year, and had learnt enough from his special subject – history – to know that the only weapon of a leader, who is not a born leader, is compromise, and that compromise, in the right hands, can become a weapon of strength. So that when his Captaincy had begun – and the Captaincy can well be an office of absolute tyranny – he had quickly understood that the only way he could retain a semblance of authority (with the two 'amiable thugs', Lansdowne and Marchant, in the Library under him) was by compromise. He compromised with every-one. When the amiable thugs suggested electing Berwick, he compromised and elected him. When he suggested electing Phillips, more to get them accustomed to the idea than from any sanguine hopes of his own, and found much

opposition to the suggestion, he compromised and postponed the idea. When Lansdowne and Marchant wanted
their *bêtes noirs* beaten, Defries compromised and beat
them. To begin with. After a while he felt quite inclined to
compromise with the system and beat victims of his own
choosing, telling himself that, after all, he was Captain.
And very soon he found himself compromising by beating
anyone anyone suggested. And, of course, he never forgot
to put on record that he found all these beatings very
painful, but one must not compromise one's sense of duty,
must one? In this way he not only compromised, but
sacrificed himself for the good of the house. The house,
particularly the tingling section of it, was ungrateful.

Defries was a short, dark, thin-shouldered, unprepossess-
ing sort of boy, who had suffered a great deal in his first
two years at Eton and now stoutly maintained that it had
done him good. More uncompromised members of the
College like Scarfe, who saw only the end product, rather
wondered.

At the beginning of the summer half Defries and
Berwick, the two remaining members of the Library, co-
opted Morgan, Pemberton and Phillips. The house in
general, and Manningham in particular, regarded the
choice of Phillips with surprise; he was rather young for
the position, one might have thought, but Defries admired
him for his occasional articles in the *Eton College Chronicle*
(Defries let it be known that he admired all creative
artists, being himself their spiritual kin) and Berwick,
after Defries's compromise in assenting to Morgan and
Pemberton, was willing, even eager, to grant a concession
in return. Phillips's position in the Library, however, was
very much one of Junior Member, and he would do well
to keep himself very much to himself. Of course, his record
collection would come in very handy for the Library
radiogram . . .

What with the new housemaster and his methods, the new Defries and his methods, and the less amiable activities of the amiable thugs, the Manningham lower boys had had a miserable spring. On their return they learnt of the new elections and there were few of them temerarious enough to hope that they would experience a particularly pleasant English summer.

Fags were being allotted, and only little 'Juggins' Partington, the ugliest and stupidest and quietest of all, who was to find himself serving Phillips, had any reason to thank his lucky stars. The poor kids! Much relief they would get from astrology!

May the Eighth at Eton College. The first day of the summer half. The tailors rub their hands and clasp their tape-measures closer round their necks. The 'Young Gentlemen', very young and officially, for the first time today, gentlemen (how Mummy would smile to hear them call me 'Sir'), have been in and out all day, biting their lips and with their little fingers picking their noses in corners, more from nervousness than stuffiness. They are very nervous; afraid chiefly that they may be incorrectly dressed. They are. Their black pin-stripe trousers are too clean, too stiff, and too well-creased to be true, and their bum-freezers (or tail-coats if they are well-grown young gentlemen) sit on them uncomfortably, not belonging, a little apologetic, like wedding-dresses on unmarried, débutante models. Fish-cakes are frying in Howard Johnson's, bangers across the road in Rowland's. Barnes Pool is as stagnant as ever this summer, and the beautiful members of 'Pop' as arrogant, strolling hand in rolled umbrella on the Eastern pavement of the High Street, incorruptible in their absolute power. They wear flowers in their button-holes of course and just occasionally with a click of two languid fingers they stop a scurrying lower boy and send him, wide-eyed and grateful, almost Japanese in his deference, up to the Post Office to buy a twopenny stamp. The sun sinks lower over School Hall and the dome of the School Library, bulging like an upturned udder, casts its shadow over the burning bush, and over the cannon in Cannon Yard. A new assistant-master, hands tucked under his gown, lopes past, measuring his strides on the paving stones, so as not to kill too many fairies, and slightly reassured by the perfunctory salutes of his pupils-to-be. If he knows how they are sizing him up, he'll be more than ever careful not to kill the fairies. He'll need them. In Alden & Blackwell's boys present their book-lists, duly signed by their housemasters. And the blotting-paper or 'blotch' they buy to faint on (put it in your shoes, hold your breath, and count to a hundred), and the ink they buy to flick each other with, and the compasses they buy to prick each other with! And their happy, smiling faces, as if they knew it all! And their evil little minds (with few exceptions)! And their clean, white collars, clean this morning! And their dirty, dirty thoughts (all but a few)!

And the sun sinks impetuously into South Meadow, and a violin sobs in the Music Schools, and the lorries of the London Brick Company rattle through the impossible streets, shaking the weary old houses to their foundations, and the violin stops in the middle of a phrase, and the notes hang expectantly over Lower Chapel, unresolved, and fade towards Windsor, unsatisfied.

Big boys and little boys, bright boys and gloomy ones, huddle into their pillows. Here and there a mouth is open, and a spot of moisture stains the linen. Here and there a pillow is throughly damp for another reason; little boys cry to God on the first night of a summer half. And bigger boys are asleep, for the most part, thankfully, for the most part, dreaming dirty. For the most part.

PART TWO

CHAPTER FOUR

DEFRIES produced the fagging list next morning in the Library with aggressive misgivings. Here could be no question of compromise, for it was traditionally his singular responsibility. The Constitution was behind him, precedent was behind him, but still he felt uncomfortable. He switched off the gramophone ('Yeah, yeah, and a yeah, yeah' it mocked him), cleared his throat, wiped his eyes, waved a bit of paper in the air.

'Aha, peace in our time,' said Morgan.

'Are you surrendering?' asked Pemberton.

'Surrendering? Why? Of course not; how can you be so gaga?' Speedwell's choice of words was something to write home (to intellectual parents) about.

'Because if you are, don't ask us for mercy.' Pemberton shot down a whole row of blindfold, enemy generals with Defries's Six Form cane. Phillips did nothing.

'Shut up, Robert,' said Berwick who couldn't wait.

'Yes, do shut up Robert,' said Morgan, the history specialist, 'in the Tower.'

'Oh, bugger up!' said Berwick.

'Shall I read through the list? No need to get steamed up, Berwick. I've given you Parsons and Beveridge.'

'Flip them!' said Berwick.

'Rather you than me,' said Pemberton, picking his nose, a habit he had not grown out of.

'A vicarious sensualist, eh, my dear chap? Library fag, Offord; Pemberton, Pearl and Gavin; Morgan, Macready and Schuster; Phillips, Partington; myself, Russell and Bigby.'

There was a pregnant pause. It seemed to last nine

months. Morgan whistled through his teeth and then stopped whistling. Berwick slowly took off his coat, rolled up his shirt-sleeve, put his lips to the crook of his elbow, and blew a raspberry. Phillips did nothing. Pemberton said incredulously:

'Russell *and* Bigby.'

'*Embarras de richesses.*'

'Russell *and* Bigby. You really are a tossed off talent-scout, you are.'

Berwick merely said scornfully: 'Parsons and Beveridge,' and began to hurl darts into the door-frame with the whole weight of his arm.

This was far worse than Defries had anticipated. He had not believed that he could get away with it totally without recriminations, but he had hoped that they would have kept it comparatively playful. But why had he chosen Russell *and* Bigby, and so provoked the others? They were both attractive certainly, but surely he was old enough now to have passed through all that. They told him in the book that it was quite natural, but only a phase, and they should know. Well, then, why? He didn't really want to touch them, he was sure he didn't, surely he didn't, sure, didn't he? Ah, to hell with them, to hell with them, to hell with the lot of them, he was the ruddy Captain and he wasn't going to touch them, any of them. Russell *and* Bigby? Why?

Morgan was taunting him in Etonian American:

'Each half we try and bring you from among the youth of today, the brightest talents, the most glamorous young stars of tomorrow. And now for your satisfaction . . .' But Defries had left the room, stupid old sod, he had a hell of a nerve, he did. A flying dart struck Phillips on the calf of his right leg and stuck there quivering.

'Well, take it out,' said Berwick, 'you're a big boy now.'

Phillips called on Scarfe soon after this, feeling rather guilty, because here he was unconverted as ever, yet all but almighty, at least in the eyes of . . . Scarfe congratulated him on his election shyly, with a muttered, 'I'm truly glad for you, Tom,' but Phillips put him at his ease ; and, feeling an excess of generosity for the stunted little guinea-pig, as well as an evanescent dissatisfaction with the scene he had just witnessed, folded up his knees, and invited the other to mess with him for the duration of the half.

'But I'm not in Debate, let alone the Library,' Scarfe had whined – he did whine a bit – 'how can I mess with you? I mean, you won't be allowed to have a tea-fag or anything.'

'Well, hell, I can make tea myself, if it comes to that, might even be able to open a tin of sardines.' And then jocularly, as if sardines had somehow brought the thought into his mind, 'And how's the evangelism?'

'Good, Tom, good. Since I've been confirmed, I don't say I've felt a different person at all, I don't mean that, but I *do* seem to have less – less resentment towards people.'

'I know.'

'I don't want to sound self-pitying or anything' (not only did he sound it, but he looked it too, very much so) 'but you know some of the horrid things they did to me last half.'

'Yes, I know.'

'Well, like when Morgan peed in my honey. I mean it was honey from the farm they'd specially sent me from home, and I couldn't really afford to *buy* any, you know. I mean Father and Mother . . .'

Oh for Chrissake, thought Phillips. But he said nothing.

'. . . Well, I don't hold it against him at all now. I mean, he probably didn't realize, you see, Tom . . .'

'No?'

'Well, no. I pray for Morgan every night now, you know. He wouldn't like it if he knew, but he needs help. I pray for you too, but of course you don't need it so much, do you? And Christ came down to save sinners . . .'

And a train rattles over the Arches towards Slough, where, on the Trading Estate, they are just beginning to work the night-shift. They have a long night before them, but many a young gentleman would gladly change places with them. And the night-shift workers, how would they react to this transposition? Just flipping ask them, that's all . . .

'. . . And I didn't pee in your honey?'

'No, of course you didn't. Why, Tom, you'll be able to share my honey now, won't you?

Good grief, thought Phillips, did I really offer to mess with him? Christmas, what the hell did I want to do that for? He said:

'Not the same lot, I hope.'

'I've got a chicken too, and a dozen new-laid eggs. I didn't bring back more than a dozen because you see they won't really last all that long in this hot weather. And then, what with the journey. And, I mean, I thought I'd probably be messing alone . . . Tom, what did you bring back?' Scarfe was obviously tring to consolidate like mad.

'I only brought my problems.' It wasn't strictly true (he had some tins of things – as a special treat a pot of Beluga caviare, but what would Scarfe know of that? – and a Fullers layer cake), but it was the kind of thing Scarfe liked to hear.

'Well, we can share them too,' said Scarfe, sprightly as ever, 'can't we?'

But: 'Why, you're a real Communist, aren't you?' And then: 'Sorry, must rush, got a French Prose,' Phillips had said and vanished. He couldn't have taken much more of that.

Scarfe sat down again at his burry and sucked away at his Conway Stewart until his lips were blue. The old oak desk was covered with inscriptions carved in the wood by generations of boys. Mostly initials and names, but high up by the side of the bookshelves someone had notched: 'Christ have mercy on us.' The guinea-pig turned his attention once more to a half-finished letter home.

. . . Tom Phillips has just asked me to mess with him, he wrote, *I'm very flattered because he's just got elected to the Library, and it's very rare for someone in the Library to mess with someone not even in Debate. It's terribly nice of him, and he's a thoroughly good person too. I am recovering from my long journey, and feel very well, in spite of a slight touch of diarrhœa . . .*

Berwick really seemed annoyed.

'What the crap are you playing at, Phillips? You have certain responsibilities when you're in the Library, don't you know, and you can't just go messing with any stinking oik you please. What the flipping hell's everyone going to think? That you've got a crush on him or something? Christ! Christ Almighty!'

'Oh, come off it, Berwick, I like the chap.'

'*Like* him? Have you seen his family? I mean have you *seen* them? He smells. Probably sleeps in his underpants for all I know. Hey, Defries, tell this oaf he can't mess with Scarfe. Hell, *I* give up.'

'Oh, my dear chap, it's not on. You must restrain these masochistic tendencies. If you want to stay in the Library, you just must mess in with the Library. It's ineluctable. Or to stretch a point at least with somebody in Debate. Don't you realize you have to set an example now? Scarfe?' It suddenly seemed to come home to him, 'Oh, my dear chap, no.'

'Look, Scarfe, I'm terribly sorry and all that, but apparently it's just not possible to mess with someone not in Debate. I'm afraid we'll have to call it off.'

'But Tom, you *said*.'

'Yes, I know I did, and I meant what I said, but I had no right to, it seems. I didn't know they'd take it so much to heart.' There was a pause in which more words seemed to be expected of him, but he really didn't think he had any more to say. He made a strange up-and-down gesture in the air, calculated, presumably, to illustrate people taking things to heart.

'But don't you see, it's too late to find someone else now.' Scarfe's voice burst in quite shrilly, as a millennium of lonely afternoons (and all the disgrace of being alone) stretched out before him, in an odd way like an airport runway. 'And what about the eggs? I offered to share my eggs with you, didn't I? They won't last a fortnight.'

But there Phillips has his opening, and he wasn't likely to waste such a unique opportunity.

'You'll just have to eat two a day,' he said, and more or less scampered from the room. For a moment he had been afraid that Scarfe would start to cry.

'But they can't expect me to live on eggs,' Scarfe said to himself unreasonably. However, he was not going to cry in spite of that suffocating lump in his throat. He was much too old to start crying over something like this. Then he remembered something else.

'Oh, why did I send that letter?' – And he burst into tears.

Mrs. Molarkey had really been a great success at her first tea-time. Presiding in the tiny kitchen, surrounded by the mysterious flames of the gas-rings, she was like a huge buddha in a lady chapel. Hands folded like a sleeping

pigeon in the warm nest of her lap. Heaving breasts like a
vast Atlantic swell. Legs like the marble pillars of a ruined
temple. And she stared out of the steam of the tea-pots like
the genie of the lamp. In the boys' eyes she was already a
'character' and, as is the habit with Eton boys, they were
very considerate towards their new servant. Some of the
smaller ones, literally overhung by her, were especially
polite. And maybe she didn't fool them with her lady
manners; and maybe, solid as she was, they could see
through her and why she had to try to be what she could
never have been, and sympathized with her for the hope-
lessness of her struggle (boys *feel* rather than understand
these things), and maybe they liked her for her size, which
maybe reminded them of childhood nannies or grannies;
or maybe not. But Mrs. Molarkey at her first tea-time had
really been a great success. On her side her feelings were
mixed. As she put it to her niece:

'Now Ai'm not saying theah not naice boys; they was
very naice to me. But they was not very naice to each
other, you know. Ai was quaite surprised to see the way
they was treating each other.'

'How, Auntie?'

'Theah words. Ai mean the things what they said,' she
checked herself; that was quite a relapse, what had come
over her – 'rude! Ai never did. And altogether not naice.'

'Poor Auntie.'

'They pushed the little ones away from the rings and
they filled theah pockets with bacon-rind, and theah was
one poor boy – not such a little one, this one – all on his
own, he was, and they took his honey away from him and
wouldn't give it back.'

'Oh dear.'

'So Ai told them to return it at once, "Return it at
once," Ai said, and they was very polite to me, and they
did. Now do you think Ai should have done thet? Was it

exceeding mai duties?' It was strange to see the lovely, white, blubbery rolls on Mrs. Molarkey's brow hoisted in self-doubt, but she was so worried she had overstepped the mark. Would a lady have acted like that? Would they have acted like that in the presence of a lady?

'Of course, Auntie,' said her niece, and smiled.

Mrs. Molarkey returned the smile, happy and trusting, and rubbed her legs vigorously as if her doubting had affected her circulation. Then she lay back in her armchair, shook it into shape, and said:

'Ai believe Sir Malcolm is conducting Tschaykovskay on the Home, mai deah. Would you be kaind enough to switch it on for me?'

'But, Auntie . . .' expostulated the niece, and then remembered. This time her aunt had made a perfectly reasonable request.

Two things had recently happened to Phillips to give him nourishing food for thought; two things of enough moment to drive out of his mind the usual memories of Jill that lurked there, ready to leap out like a monster hiding in a cave when things seemed quietest. Yet it was only now in the middle of the night that he had a chance thoroughly to chew them over. Firstly there was the easy thing: his election to the Library.

His immediate reaction to the hordes that had swarmed in and trampled him down had been that the whole world had gone mad and decided to do away with all Phillipses (he had always had a deep-rooted fear of something of the sort; a lot of people have). And then, while they had scattered the clothes from his ottoman in fanatical disarray, he had recognized the symptoms and had seen them as if from another planet, with joy throbbing against his heart and beneath it a jabbing of guilt; for did he deserve this kind of honour? He was very young and childish in some ways. What about, well what about those nights when he tossed and turned and relived in an agony of spirit the moments when he had caressed the girl from Shiplake Lock (not such very lurid moments however he remembered them)? What about the times when he had degraded her in his mind and with his body while she, totally innocent of it all, had written such plaintive letters full of the tennis team and the absurd idiosyncrasies of the Mademoiselle? Was that behaviour worthy of a member of the Library? He would have to reform. Because now it appeared that by the new year he would surely be Captain of the House and have its moral and physical well-being in his hands, and if his hands were dirty . . . Captain of the House. In 'stick-ups' and bow-tie. Perhaps even in Pop . . . And he couldn't see a member of Pop doing anything degrading. And yet people had talked about Hamilton and the waitress at the Gay Adventure. But people would always talk, always be nasty, lying gossips, like washerwomen. And then there had been the rumours of Proctor-Hayworth, whom they had christened the Pop Tart; but there would always be rumours – jealousy probably. Who knows? Of course you probably had temptations just the same if you were in Pop; check trousers and coloured waistcoats weren't exactly monks' habits. But he couldn't imagine any of them actually . . . Anyway, it wasn't his business, and he would do better to go to sleep than to lie awake scandal-mongering. He was much calmer now; the heart-felt joy and the nagging guilt had worn off, and he was left with a pleasurable anticipation of the weeks to come. There'd be records to play, and boy-calls to make, and he'd probably even have a fag. He could hardly wait for that. He felt himself actively happy, for the first time in four years at Eton; it was a nice feeling.

But the other thing was not easy to understand

3*

especially as he was growing sleepier, and altogether less rational every minute. It was a simple enough occurrence in itself. The house-cat, a smelly, emasculated creature with eczema and epilepsy, had caught a young bird in the house garden. It must have been tormenting it for some time before Phillips had noticed them from his window and had thrown a stone which had caught the cat on the side of the head and driven it away. He had then rescued the bird, an unfledged hedge-sparrow he thought, and brought it to his room. It was not badly hurt, but part of the neck was bare to the crop. As he lay in bed he could hear it scuffling on his hot-water bottle in a corner of the room, unused probably to the loneliness. He had fed it milk through an eye-dropper, but could hardly hope that the bird would survive the night. He turned over in bed, pressed his hands between his knees, drifted a little farther from rationalization. What could it all mean? Cat and bird? Tom and Jerry? The Hunter and the Hunted? Was this a Symbolical Experience with a Message for him if only he could Understand? But of course it was happening all over the world. Every minute of the hour, every hour of the day, every day. Siamese cats and Persian cats and Manx cats. All chasing, hunting, teasing, feathery bundles of birds. A universal holocaust. There should be a United Nations Sub-Committee to inquire . . . And he floated off into a troubled dreamful sleep.

'Long time no see,' said the Bishop, who was on a visit to the school to check that no wolves had crept in among his tidily branded flock, 'what's the news from the front lines?'

'Nothing good,' said Scarfe disconsolately.

'Come now, surely the army of the Lord is not faint-hearted? Has it not taken captive any prisoners yet?'

'No, sir.' They were talking in Scarfe's room. The 'Childhood of Raleigh' and 'Queen Elizabeth II' looked

down on them from the walls, the old world and the new.
There was also an oil-painting of some slimy-looking
fishing-boats on some slimy-looking mud-flats as seen
through (and here was a daring sop to modernistic
symbolism) fishing nets! It was a picture that Scarfe's
mother had given him – though heaven knows how she
had got hold of it – on his first leaving for Eton. How
embarrassed he had been at Waterloo because it was too
big to fit into his suitcases! Prominent on the bookshelves
were C. S. Lewis's *Screwtape Letters*, some old copies of
Readers' Digest and a presentation volume of Queen
Victoria's favourite poet.

'Ah, well, the Lord is patient. He sees the strivings of the
just. By the way, you haven't had any more trouble *that*
way, have you?'

Scarfe blushed and shook his head.

'Good boy. I'm glad to hear it. Playing games hard, of
course?'

'Quite. Rowing a bit.'

'Mmm, good. Very glad to hear it. Used to be a dry-bob
myself. Did Chinamen.' How Morgan would have raised
his eyebrows over that! 'Once before an M.C.C. match
bowled out Jack Hobbs in the nets. But of course he said he
wasn't ready.'

'Help me, sir!' said Scarfe suddenly.

'What with, Chinamen? Well, it's all a question of grip,
you see.'

'No, with Phillips. He's the one I thought I had converted last half. I mean, he seemed to be.'

'And now?' the Bishop prompted. He mustn't be long.
The Chaplain's eldest daughter had been having a series
of early nights. He stood over Scarfe, legs apart, between
him and the light, like a huge shadow creeping up the
wall. Scarfe explained how Phillips had been elected to
the Library, and was becoming unapproachable.

'I had hoped that he and I together, the two of us, with the help of the Lord that is, might form a kind of outpost and really do good works in the house. We could do so much him and me.'

'Only one thing for it,' said the Bishop impatiently, seeking for an exit line, 'you must Get Him Alone. Good luck, old son.'

No son of mine, the Bishop reflected to himself as he sped along the Eton Wick Road towards his room. He didn't know what was happening to Etonians these days. They were becoming morbidly introspective and, as to their voices and general manner, well they might be just anybody. And to think of this tedious creature, Scarfe, in the light blue and black. Fancy trying to inflict his sordid little troubles on a Bishop with claims on his time; where was the boy's self-respect? Even a curate would hardly dare . . . But that was the trouble with being a Bishop; the awful dreariness of ninety per cent of the sinners one had to deal with. The really colourful ones never seemed eager to come to him. Strange.

Scarfe trotted bravely into prayers, wondering how on earth he would be able to Get Phillips, so elevated now, Alone. But somehow it must be done. A Bold Plan began to ferment in his brain.

Manningham lay back in the bath and let the water rise over his hirsute belly. Not a bad belly for a man of thirty-eight. Hard and smooth as Cheddar cheese. He patted it with his hands until the water splashed over the side of the bath. Well, he thought, they couldn't be such a bad lot of boys. After all, they never knew just when he might be coming round and, although he always knocked, he never waited for an answer. And yet tonight they had none of them even looked guilty.

But of course it was a warm night.

He wasn't sure at all whether he ought to let Phillips keep the bird. Animals were strictly forbidden, but after Henley, for instance, one usually turned a blind eye to goldfish. And then again with Phillips in the Library and the Captain of the House Apparent, it would never do to make an enemy of him. He believed that Phillips respected him and the boy was generous-natured. Just think of the letter that the Dame had unearthed in his burry. From a typically stupid little girl, but moving in its way. Manningham looked down at his body lying flaccid in the bath and sighed. What a waste! Still, that was a familiar feeling to him and he quickly banished it from his mind. Phillips could keep the bird (if he *could*) but must not regard it as anything but a magnanimous exception. He would make that perfectly clear.

Manningham pulled the plug out with his toes, changed his mind, and blocked the waste-pipe with his heel. Defries was becoming a problem. He surely should know by now the folly of choosing those two particular boys to fag for him. He had always seemed so amenable to public opinion, and now, here he was, deliberately it seemed, flouting it. He surely could not be ignorant of what people would be saying. Defries had seemed such a steady boy too, but you simply never knew how power would affect the most level-headed people. I mean, look at the war.

Manningham towelled himself vigorously, almost like a flagellant, and thought for a while about Danton, whom he had made the subject of a special study at Oxford. How awful to be murdered in the bath! Life and dignity at once surrendered. Like his poor Aunt Celia, the circumstances of whose death (his parents had discussed them in whispers when they thought him asleep) had shocked him so deeply as a child. Pray God he would die in bed. And be cremated. Manningham dried with fastidious care between his toes, being nervous of athlete's foot. Not that he thought there was anything suspicious about Defries's relationships with his fags – or ever would be; curiously, though the intelligent boys preached an awful lot, it was generally, in his experience, the dumber ones who did the practising. Russell and Bigby. Quite good families, both (not that *that* was any criterion). But steady families. Bigby got his looks from his mother presumably; Russell, God only knew. Some under-the-stairs work there perhaps! Well, all in all, he was glad he didn't have a houseful of monsters. Old Naylor used to turn down pretty boys; and much good it did him too!

But how stupid of Defries! How could an intelligent boy come to be so stupid? It surely wasn't that he was arrogant. Manningham climbed into his faded, striped pyjamas. How clever he had been not to comment on Pemberton's reading matter. An illustrated Rabelais! Always wisest to be discreet, these language blokes had such strange set books. Come to think of it, it was odd that they should take such pains to edit Juvenal and Tacitus and Suetonius, and all the while the language specialists . . . *Manon Lescaut* and *Madame Bovary*, Baudelaire, Rabelais and Zola; there was obviously only one way to become a classic writer in France. Disgusting nation! And Morgan, Pemberton's friend, that was an odd twosome. And it wasn't just Morgan's choice of friends that was odd. Morgan! The one boy he could never understand. The only one who inevitably called him 'Sir', not ironically at all; quietly and respectfully, at the end of every sentence. Christ, just once he wished he wouldn't!

Manningham curled up and went to sleep. He always slept curled up. Ever since, at the age of eight, he had shared a bed for a week with his elder sister.

CHAPTER FIVE

A WEEK passed and Phillips, to the gratification of his colleagues in the Library, assiduously avoided Scarfe. It was not difficult. Scarfe of course had no right of entry into the Library and Phillips took good care that much of his time was spent there. At boys' dinner the Library sat alone with Manningham and any old boys who were flash enough to have a sports car and a débutante to show off at their old school. In College Chapel they sat opposite each other, but Scarfe was too pious to take advantage of that, and in any case, the religious gloom made positive identification at any distance extremely tricky. And at work they had no intercourse because Scarfe was a mathematician, Phillips a linguist. And so it was that the only time Scarfe could hope to Get Phillips Alone was after nine-thirty in the evening when all boys – whoever they were – were confined to their rooms; but he also knew that to call on another boy at that time was tantamount to calling on your Maker – or at least on the Headmaster, which was a more immediately awesome proposition. However, he *must* see him. The Bishop had said so. And for Scarfe, although he was not yet fully aware of it, his motives in wishing to Get Phillips Alone were complicated by a new feeling. Ever since Phillips had been elevated to the Library, Scarfe had looked up to him with something amounting almost to idolatry. It was natural in Scarfe, who spoke certainly no more than a dozen words a day in confidence to anyone, to turn in his loneliness to the person who had once deliberately come to him for advice. In Scarfe's eyes Phillips was all-sufficient. His articles in the *Chronicle* were so witty (though to a less biased critic they were heavy-handed and self-conscious to an extreme), his mind was so versatile (*Moby Dick* and *Pride and Prejudice* were on the shelf above *his* bed), his attainments were so varied (wasn't he, for instance, a real golfer with a genuine grown-up handicap?) that Scarfe completely failed to understand how anyone could treat Phillips with as scant respect as did Pemberton and Morgan, Defries – in spite of their literary empathy – and Berwick. At meals, when the others were being particularly brutish about passing him the vegetables, Scarfe, who had lost his appetite anyway, turned his burning, brown eyes to Phillips, sitting frostily at the top-table, and forgot his unhappiness.

To everyone's surprise Phillips's hedge-sparrow survived the week. Not only survived but flourisheld A little turkey-starter or some Marie biscuit on the end of the dropper, and the bird was pecking away as greedily as a king. A little milk or water in the dropper, and it couldn't open its yellow beak wide enough. Inevitably, though, some of the food would drop on to its neck and chest, and here the young feathers became bedraggled, lost their sheen, since the bird was still too young to preen itself, and fell out. The little head with its angry, bright eyes seemed sometimes to be stuck at the end of a stalk as it swivelled round three hundred and sixty degrees, and when it slept with its head tucked away under its wing, it was possible to see beyond the crop almost to the guts. And this was strange; that very soon Phillips's attraction for and tenderness towards the little bird (and he still fed it regularly every couple of hours or so despite the inconvenience, adding drops of calcium to the food to strengthen the beak and claws) turned to a kind of disgust, so much so that sometimes, especially in the mornings, he was hardly able to approach the makeshift cage without his gorge rising. It was the smell that troubled him and the green stains on the newspapers, but it was more than this too, something elemental in him that made him wish each morning that the thing had not lasted out another night. And at the same time the bird seemed to come to recognize him and would welcome him vociferously when he came in and sit on his shoulder and investigate his ears and display his love in other more enduring ways. Such loyalty of affection (he was nervous of anyone else) was strange in so young a bird.

The Colours Test is a vicious institution which does a necessary job atavistically well. At American schools there is generally a period of 'orientation', in which newcomers are helped to find their way round their new society. At Eton, far from being orientated by a kindly or considerate mentor, they are coldly informed that after a fortnight (or sometimes three weeks) they will be examined on the topography, political hierarchy and social observances of the school. They will need to know the different 'colours' of the twenty-five houses ('brown and mauve quarters', 'scarlet with a black skull and cross-bones', etc.), they will need to know the precise location of each house, each geographical landmark, each traditional meeting-place. They will need to know, for example, how best to reach Mesopotamia from 'Sixth-form Bench', or how long it would take a desperate fag to run from 'Poets' Walk' to the 'Copper Horse'. They will need to know the initials of each housemaster and the name of the building in which he lives. They will need to know everything that the Captain of the House considers that they need to know, and that is only a beginning. If they pass their test – with flying colours so to speak – they are then considered responsible enough and are privileged to run errands for Library and Debate and undertake the many other duties of the Eton fag. If they fail, they may or may not be given a second chance, and will probably be beaten. As a form of orientation the Colours Test could not perhaps be bettered.

It was the night of Sunday, 29th May. The three new boys stood still and pale as wax-works outside the Library door and opposite Mrs. Molarkey's door. Each of them was running over in his mind – and mouthing with his lips – names and numbers, patterns, initials, and stripes in a last despairing attempt to marshal into some kind of order the broken kaleidoscope of his brain. From the Library radiogram came the resonant and implacable chords of Tschaikovsky's First Piano Concerto.

'Why do you play that record?' Phillips asked greenly. Defries smiled.

'It's a kind of call to arms. Has much the same psychological effect, we hope, as the roll of drums before the guillotine.'

'Don't you feel,' said Pemberton, 'that this music tugs terribly at your nerve ends? Don't you find that it's like a . . . like a plectrum on the heart-strings?'

'Yes, exactly. We must instill into them a sense of Occasion; we must make them feel, well, wanted.'

'And are they?' asked Morgan.

'Well, they had better not have been slack that's all.' Berwick was always the one for essentials. 'What the hell are we waiting for? Let's do a flipping brace for Christ's sake.'

Morgan repeated thoughtfully: 'Let's do a flipping brace for Christ's sake. Okay. Why not?'

But the new boys were not slack. They were very stalwart and unswerving, these new boys. They were not to be panicked or brow-beaten and to the questions that were hurled at them, they paused, and gave considered answers. Phillips, whenever possible, posed an easy question (where's the Leg of Mutton Pond? Everyone knew that), but Berwick began to interrupt Phillip's

questions with more demanding ones of his own devising.
Technically each had to score seventy-five per cent to
pass the test. After twenty minutes only one of them, a
molish, inky-fingered little chap, had dropped a few
points. Defries dismissed the other two who chorused:
'Thank you, sir,' and scuttled off like electric hares, then
pulled down a length of bamboo from the wall.

'Do you know what this is?' he asked.

'*God* knows,' Morgan added helpfully with a kind smile.

The boy was either very short-sighted, very stupid or
very brave, because he blinked (behind the goggles) and
inquired:

'What did you say? Sorry.' Of course alternatively it's
possible that he could have been very deaf.

'You will be sorry.' Berwick looked at him out of the
tops of his eyes.

'The cane?'

'Yes, but what kind of cane?' In fact it was the 'Sixth
Form Cane', slightly longer than the ordinary variety.
Defries, being in the Sixth Form, was privileged to use
this one.

'I don't know.'

'You fail,' said Berwick, crumpling up the score-sheet,
and letting it flutter to the ground. Phillips bent and
picked it up.

'He's got one more question to come,' he said, 'where is
Jack's?'

'Between the Parade Ground and the fives courts.'

'Fifteen out of twenty,' said Phillips smoothing the paper
and passing it to Defries. Berwick snorted, but there was
nothing to be done. The Library, being a body politic,
must not be seen to disagree. So he snorted. Defries saw
the time had come for compromise.

'Don't think,' he said, swishing the cane, 'don't imagine
just because you've scraped home that you've commenced

your school career on a particularly auspicious note. Don't believe that you have in any respect recommended yourself to us by the slip-shod, casual way you've gone about your work since you arrived here. There is no place in m'tutor's for inky slackers, and, if you don't mind your manners, and – and get some pumice-stone to your fingers, you'll get what's coming to you before you've even seen it come. Now get out!'

The boy choked out: 'Yes, sir,' and made for the door. Pemberton languidly extended a foot and the new boy went head-first into the panelling which splintered.

'Now look what you've done,' said Pemberton, 'you do ask for it, don't you?'

When the tearful fellow had blundered out of the room, they all turned on Phillips furiously. He sat quite innocently upright, hands on knees as if at any minute they might leap up with a life of their own and chase each other round the room. And then a strange pause ensued; everyone knew the assault was about to be launched but, like the gentlemen they were, they each stood aside for the others to begin. Defries it was who gathered from the silence that they owed it to his seniority and so accordingly:

'I must say, Phillips, to put it mildly,' enunciated Defries with the greatest clarity, 'I must say, old chap, I find it most reprehensible in you to disagree with a member of the Library in front of a Lower Boy. If you are to remain a member of the Library, you are going to have to change your ideas.' Phillips, who was beginning to wonder if he could have been wrong, moved over to the window to get help from Nature.

'Oh, now you've upset him . . .' broke in Pemberton.

'I was the one who proposed your election, you know, old boy; I begin to think I was guilty of a bad miscalculation.'

'Speaking for myself,' said Berwick, 'I think it's ruddy bad form.' He had decided to retain a dignified silence on the subject but his grievances had proved too much for his dignity. 'You really are a b.f.,' he elaborated.

Phillips: 'But you were being purely sadistic . . .'

'Purely?' asked Morgan.

'Trust you,' said Pemberton.

'Would you really?' said Morgan.

'He knew his stuff, and you had no right to beat him when—'

'Who was going to beat him?' asked Defries. 'There you go, jumping to conclusions, my dear chap. I was going to frighten him.'

'First,' said Pemberton.

'Now, look,' Defries was thoroughly roused, angry. All these interruptions. How could he assert his authority? 'First, you try and lower the dignity of the Library by messing with a flipping oik, then you try and interfere with the Captain in the performance of his duties—'

'No, you really shouldn't interrupt a man in the performance of his duties, should you?' Pemberton asked in his understanding voice.

'It's vulgar,' said Morgan, siding with Pemberton. Defries had lost control of his anger now, and found himself quite unable to pick up where he had left off:

'Well, all I can say is that you're a bloody nuisance and – and you've just about cooked your goose.'

'And we have other fish to fry, so there!' said Pemberton.

'Oh, be quiet Pemberton,' snapped Defries.

'Sorry, sir, I was only—'

'You heard what the gentleman said,' from Morgan who was leaning against the mantelpiece, and tearing pages from an old schools copy of *Hamlet*, 'wrap up, otherwise the gentleman may lose his temper with you.'

Pemberton smiled at Morgan, a conspiratorial smile, but Morgan looked quite grave. Morgan smiled seldom; just occasionally when he was on his own, and at the strangest things . . .

It was the bane of Defries's life that whenever he got warmed to a cause about which he felt strongly, the others reduced the whole thing to a farce, and he was left clinging to his fading argument, like the boy with his thumb in the breached dyke. And, always, inevitably, the water came pouring in over his head. It wasn't a bit fair. A gentleman had a right to lose his temper sometimes.

That night Scarfe, feeling perhaps that God would be most likely to be with him because it was Sunday, determined to Act. He had to see Phillips, had to speak with him alone and undisturbed, it was really as simple as that because, if he saw him, spoke to him, well then anything might happen. He waited until nine-thirty, then waited another five minutes before making any move, and then counted to seventy-seven for no real reason except that he didn't want to rush into anything before he was ready, and then defiantly slipped into his rather shabby camel-hair dressing-gown, grabbed a towel to excuse himself if he should be questioned on the way, and pattered up and along to Phillips's room. Phillips was sitting at his burry with an open exercise-book in front of him, in which he had written:

SUNDAY QUESTIONS   T. A. Phillips
I. St. Augustine
 The thing that impresses me most about St. Augustine's teachings . . .

before becoming utterly depressed by the tedium of the subject. Scarfe tapped twice at the door – softly with the

metacarpals like a neighbour come to borrow something –
and came in rather quickly. His little round button-head
was redder than ever and in his brown eyes there was a
gleam, rather more conciliatory than evangelistic.

'Hello, Tom,' he said.

Phillips looked up in total astonishment. 'What on
earth?'

'Well, you never speak to me at all now, and I mean I
just had to see you and speak to you, and this was the only
time I could be sure of catching you in.' He smiled happily
at the success of his little plot. 'I knew you'd be sapping
away at something. What are you looking at me like that
for, Tom?'

'Well, in heaven's name, don't you expect to be looked
at. You know what'll happen to you if you're found in
here at this time? You know what'll happen to me too?
You know that Mockingbird hasn't been round yet this
evening?'

'Well, yes, but you see I don't mean any harm, and
we'll hear him coming, and I only wanted to know how
things were in the Library, and – and, I mean, how things
were with you, Tom?'

'And I think you must be out of your mind if you call
round now just to inquire after my health.'

'We're opposite each other in Chapel; did you know
that?'

Phillips had noticed. 'No, I really can't say I had
noticed. Now look, Scarfe, for your own good, might I
suggest—'

'*My* good, Tom?'

'Well, what the hell else?'

'No, I didn't come for my good, Tom. I came to see
how the Work was progressing.'

'Work?'

'You know, Tom, don't be silly. The work of the Lord.

What's it like in the Library? I mean are you doing good with them?'

Phillips breathed deeply: 'Now look, Scarfe, I *may* have given you the impression of encouraging you when you came round before, but that was at a reasonable hour, and I wasn't in the Library then, and –well, I was younger.'

'You mean you don't *care* any more?' Scarfe brought this out with such tragic emphasis that it was all Phillips could do to avoid laughing – the whole thing was bloody ridiculous – 'You mean just because of a few paltry bastards like that' – Scarfe was really roused now, he'd hardly ever even so much as thought a word like that before – 'you're willing to give up everything we had striven for together. You, Tom, I thought you were different from the others.'

'Just a moment—' To be lectured to by this, this, this curmudgeon! He would lose all his self-respect in a minute.

'Yes, we had striven together, deny it all you like. You'd prayed with me once, don't say you've forgotten that.'

And it was quite horribly true that he had. It had been towards the end of last half one sultry Sunday afternoon – the sort when Nature and reality seem both suspended – and Scarfe had come running in, just like that, abrupt as anything, and had said:

'Will you join me in a short prayer for the unconverted?'

Hell, it was like drinking a toast to yourself!

But caught off guard, he had been too embarrassed to think of a reply, and, to his own extreme amazement, had complied. He shivered with horror now as he thought of it. But a joke was a joke.

'I don't care what I did once, do you hear? I shit every day, but there's no reason why I should join you in that.'

Scarfe went deathly pale. His hands were shaking so much that he had to thrust them into the pockets of his

dressing-gown. It seemed almost as though he might have
a fit.

'You bastard! You cheap bastard!' he shouted at the
top of his voice. Unwisely.

Manningham, who was making his nightly tour, stopped
in his tracks and – though there was no one watching
him – raised his eyebrows in astonishment. Then without
running, because obviously it would not do to run, he
quick-marched, delicately on the points of his patent-
leather toes, along the corridor, to meet in full career,
blindly head down, charging like rabid cavalry, a trembling bundle of camel-hair misery, that was the boy Scarfe.
Manningham, who prided himself fishily on his sang-
froid, merely wrinkled his forehead in distaste and said:

'Go straight to your room, Scarfe. When your family
expect so much from you, it is very foolish and ungrateful
of you to behave in this manner.'

Phillips returned to St Augustine and sat in front of him
guiltily and unhappily for some minutes before crossing
out what he had written, and substituting:

*The thing that depresses me most about St. Augustine's
teachings* . . .

Manningham completed his tour and then went to run
his bath. Scarfe, in his confusion and his dressing-gown,
did not return to his room.

The Bishop had once told him: 'If ever you feel like a
man-to-man chat, old son, and I happen to be in Eton at
the time, do look me up, won't you? At the Chaplain's
house, you know.' This was an old formula of his, calculated to inspire trust and confidence. He had learnt by
happy experience that very few boys took him up on it;
most of them would rather whisper their secrets to the
reeds than have their backs sympathetically slapped by

the muscular Bishop. Even in his Liverpool boys' clubs
many of the intimate confidences to which he listened with
such tolerant wisdom and such prurient Christian understanding had come straight out of American *Confession*
magazines. But in Liverpool the lack for so many years of
facilities for field or track sports has inevitably led to other
improvisations . . .

Scarfe went running through the night, his dressing-
gown swishing after him like phosphorescent wake behind
a chunky motor-boat. It was almost dark, probably as dark
as it ever would be at the end of May, but the night air and
the darkness parted to let him through. He was puffing
and panting and sweat was prickling on his forehead and
running into his eyes and down his cheeks. Past the black
and white Tudor front of Evans's House (it flashed past
him like a keyboard) and, whoosh!, across the High Street,
oblivious of the consternation he caused to an impression-
able lady motorist from residential Windsor, across Long
Walk and School Yard. The cobbles bruise his feet and
jar his spine, and the founder frightens him, looming up,
green and gaga, out of the past. His piston arms are
pumping just as furiously now and bodkins prick and
prance inside his legs. And through his befuddled brain,
which feels as if it is rattling like a withered walnut in its
shell, run no thoughts of the sacred rules he is breaking.
To be out after lock-up, without a house-ticket, in his
night-clothes. He might as well have opened a cat-house
in Common Lane or sold out School Office to the Pari-
mutuel. Finally he flings himself at the Bishop's door and
collapses on the ground, as the door yields before him.
There he sprawls like a silly, big fish, cast up in a storm,
heaving and retching and stupid as he sees the Bishop,
kneeling on the basin, stretching and craning his neck as
the near-naked Chaplain's daughter glides out of his field
of vision.

From that moment on Scarfe's religion was an entirely more cynical and practical—and sensible—affair.

Six days to go till 4th June. Which means that for the more longsighted of the boys the best Eton suit is now at the cleaners. Top-hats are being taken out from under beds or from on top of sock-cupboards to be brushed within inches of their silken lives for this, the one day in their year. Those with White Tickets for idleness, slackers, lags, visionaries, who consequently have all leave automatically stopped until they regain favour, are driven almost frantic with worry – except the visionaries. Chances are that they haven't written the bad news home for shame (for shame!) and they dream about armies of relatives marching in strict column of threes out of the family Rolls only to find that young Rupert is not available. 'But Rupert, darling, why didn't you write and tell us?' Uncle Henry behind his hand to Uncle William: 'Young buggers today got no guts!' Housemasters with appointment books coming out of their bindings, wrestle with the careers of Cabinet Ministers in *Who's Who*. Mustn't suggest Trinity to Lord Smeltenham; mustn't suggest Balliol to the Earl of Rossiter; mustn't suggest the regular army to Canon Plumpton; mustn't suggest the Church to Sir Samuel Josephs.

Caterers, pyrotechnicians, worry themselves insomniac over the proper blending of tradition with innovation. Gossip-writers sharpen their pencils on their tongues; their claws and their teeth almost whittled away by continual use; lots of lovely white débutante necks to bite into this year. Watch the blue blood flow! Chelsea garages pep up tired T.R.s and inject everything but cod-liver oil into the tormented works. Poor but honest parents – two rare virtues in this society – make trips to Covent Garden; not the Opera, not the Ballet, not the vegetable market.

Mining-socialist fathers of Etonian sons buy bags of false hair and sink themselves in spirit-gum. Younger sisters everywhere buy their first brassières; Daddy is probably not informed. Elder sisters buy new dresses; Daddy, warned beforehand, signs the cheque, choking over his Bisque d'Homard. The fine spell of weather breaks, and the rains set in. Everyone grows restless. Younger boys, who have not seen it all before, lie awake at night; old ones, who have seen it all too many times, try and forget in their Kensington pied-à-terres. The boats are finally chosen, crews briefed, hopes shattered.

Truly it's a unique occasion; unique and depressingly predictable like a pancake race.

Defries lay back in the one armchair in his room, his head sunk on the bridge of his finger-tips. His oily, attenuated face with the rather petulant mouth took on in repose a sulky expression, but the eyes were always quick and bright. The whole effect, in as much as it was like anything, was like that of a bad-tempered, hung-over satyr. He was watching Bigby turning back his bed, puffing up the pillow, smoothing out the sheets. Bigby was good at this, having frequently watched the parlourmaid doing it at home; the incongruity did not strike him. He was one of those angel-faced boys who seem inexplicably to increase and flourish like pimpernels in the English Public Schools. Very blond, but not as blond as he had been, with mischief in his eyes and a Cupid mouth, he was so sentimental in appearance that old ladies (and old gentlemen, too very often) would look after him in the streets, and rough boys would shout rude words as if he really were an angel or something. Furthermore, he was unusual in that both he and his clothes were invariably immaculate, he showed half an inch of shirt-cuff (except when he stretched for something) and his trouser-crease

broke just on his polished shoe. His parting was as
inevitably straight as a Roman road – but with a little
curve into the slope right at the end – and, when he blew
his nose, which was seldom, he unfolded a clean handker-
chief with infinite care beforehand. But whether he was
angelic in fact, or whether he used his face, like Queen
Victoria's waxed smile, to hide his true feelings, nobody –
not even his family – knew. His mother naturally was on
the side of the angels and no evidence had as yet come to
light to prove her prejudice unwarranted. Defries also
was one of the ones who wondered.

'Tell me,' he said, 'what private school did you grace?'

'Heathfields.'

'Did you learn much there?'

'About what?' A fair, unobjectionable question. But
there was a coldness of intonation that – well, maybe not.

'Of things in general.'

'No, I learnt more about things in particular.'

'What sort of things?'

'Latin, Greek, French, History, you know.'

'Did they say anything to you when you left?' Bigby
opened his beautiful, blue eyes extra wide.

'They said good-bye.' It was not cheeky; or was it?
Defries could make no complaint.

'But didn't they say anything about Life?'

'The Scripture Master said that life wasn't only for
living. I don't remember anything else.'

'Well, look, if you have any problems, or questions you'd
like to ask or anything of that sort, just come to me.'

'Is that all for me tonight?'

'Oh yes, run along, and remember what I said.'

'Good night, Defries.'

'Good night, Bigby.'

Defries spent a few minutes in pleasant meditation. He
was day-dreaming really. Damn it, he thought suddenly,

it's my duty isn't it? The welfare of the house is in my keeping, as Manningham told me. It's a great responsibility. And ignorance is one of the forces against which I must struggle.

Defries really believed this. He wasn't fooling himself at all; hardly.

It is only very rarely that Eton housemasters take the law into their own hands and deal out corporal punishment themselves. And this is because 'screwing', as it is called, seems to a housemaster rather like displaying a lack of confidence in the ordinary processes of house government. For extreme cases 'floggings' on the flogging block (*such a favourite with the tourists*) are administered by the Headmaster or Lower Master, and for blatant offences in the streets, for instance, or on the cricket-field, there's the grim ritual known as 'Pop-tanning', in which one cut of the cane for each member of Pop is inflicted on the drone victim. Add to these processes the far more common 'beatings-up', delivered by house captains, games captains and senior members of the Corps in their respective houses, and it becomes apparent that the incidence of 'screwing' must of necessity be small. When out of a school population of under twelve hundred perhaps sixty boys wield the cane and when the Headmaster and Lower Master swing the birch to great effect, most housemasters let them get on with it, and add nothing to the general swishing tumult all around them.

And in passing, who can argue that, from these sixty boys and thirty masters who find themselves flogging the hell out of a recalcitrant child, there will be many who abuse that privilege? No, in any given year there will be but a handful of abuses. And who would maintain that even such abuses as do arise from time to time are of any importance when set against a system that produces so high a proportion of, say, our incorruptible parliamentary leaders. And if they in their turn sometimes seem thick-skinned, then their childhood discipline which hardened their bottoms for sitting on government benches, may in part seem to blame; but how often does a thick skin hide a sensitive spirit? – and we must not criticize this or that minister because he subordinates his aesthetic sensibilities to the cares of state.

In the case of Scarfe, Manningham found himself uncertain as to the best course to adopt. Stratton with his usual unquestioning benevolence had accepted the boy as guinea-pig, and Manningham had the responsibility for two more years. It had been generally agreed among the staff that the few grammar-school boys from improvident homes should be treated much as the others ('what have we to fear?' one had remarked, 'we can rely on the boys to keep them down' – as if he were talking of a particularly nasty form of black-fly) but that, wherever possible, scandals in which such boys were involved, should be avoided. 'Publicity on this subject,' the Headmaster pronounced, 'might be the last thing we want.' By accepting a minority of non-fee-paying oppidans a useful argument had been developed against the provocations of 'liberal' do-gooders, or the jealous attacks of the down-trodden masses – assuming they ever found their spokes-man. And, by limiting that minority, it had been insured that the rarified air of Eton College should not be seriously polluted, except when the wind came blowing in from Slough, and there was nothing to be done about that. 'We must not become a Strontium Society,' the Headmaster had added cryptically. On the whole, therefore, Manning-ham decided that it must be best to leave disciplinary action to Defries and the Library. He could rely on them to eschew any effeminate leniency for what was, after all, not only a very severe offence, but also a very demoralizing one for the house in general. He could just hear some of his colleagues crowing: 'Unlike at Manningham's where it seems they make a practice of nocturnal perambulating...' It was extremely fortunate for Manningham's peace of mind that he knew nothing of Scarfe's visit to the Bishop.

When the housemaster explained the position to him, Defries quite understood, and promised to be unremittingly severe in his punishment of Scarfe. 'You have my authority,' Manningham went on, 'to act as you think best in the interests of morality and discipline and you have my unstinted support and approval in advance.' Defries had smiled and replied: 'Thank you, sir. That's very magnanimous of you.'

Phillips's disgust with the hedge-sparrow slowly wore off. It had been a reaction similar to that a mother may experience towards her baby soon after birth, or an author towards a completed work (where the post-natal depression is inevitable in most cases), a *self*-disgust as much as anything. Because, unless one is a narcissist, inevitably one feels, not every day but frequently, a physical loathing of the processes of the body, an objective sickness that one is what one is because one does what one does. And one wants to *be* it, but would much rather not *do* it. And the resignation to, or victory over, this problem is what is often meant by 'coming to terms with oneself'. An anatomy lecture is all very well but we grow pale at our first operation; soon, of course, we acquire the necessary medical callousness or professionalism, and the patient under the sheet climbs back on to the blackboard. So, in a smaller way, Phillips came to terms with the hedge-sparrow and began to delight in lifting it high above his head with its claws nervously clasped about his middle-finger (almost as tightly as a baby clasps), until, summoning its courage, it hardened its grip, half unwrapped its wings (think of a high-diver swinging his arms on the edge of the board), and launched itself into space to flutter desperately round and round, losing height but gaining confidence until it came to rest, gratefully, on the edge of the table or dug its claws into depressing St. Augustine.

Certainly the bird was growing stronger. It could now take its own food and drink from saucers (which saved Phillips no end of trouble) and, when it ruffled the feathers on the back of its neck, they fell back shining into place. No longer was the flickering of the nictitating membrane visible and the beak and claws had toughened and calcified.

Morgan and Pemberton had always shown an unlikely interest in the progress of the bird and had even taken upon themselves some of the duties of its upbringing. Phillips had neither encouraged nor discouraged them; but he was both suspicious and jealous of their attentions. On Monday morning, 30th May, the morning after Scarfe's escapade, he made for the door as soon as they came into his room. Pemberton had a caterpillar with him, held tightly, like something that smells, between finger and thumb. If the sparrow could be persuaded to eat a caterpillar, they could be pretty certain that he would survive. Morgan intervened between Phillips and the door and said:

'Just a moment. News most pressing, my dread lord, from the duke.'

Phillips at once feared the worst. He knew from experience that when Morgan began to put on voices, he was relishing the moment, and when he relished the moment, it usually meant that somebody was in trouble. Not that you could ever be sure with Morgan. Now Phillips could not be certain of what had happened to Scarfe the previous night after his precipitous flight into the corridor. He had heard – as he thought – Manningham's voice, and doubted whether Scarfe, in his highly emotional state, had been able to bluff his way out of a compromising position. He had stayed in his room tugging at his corn-coloured hair until Manningham's disdainful monotone and the pattering of Scarfe's slippers on the stairs had both died away, and so he had seen nothing of the encounter. But it could hardly have been a comfortable one. Pemberton's next words did little to reassure him.

'Have you ever attended a beating-up session?'

'No. Only my own.'

'Where you were not aesthetically objective. He hasn't lived, has he? How do you think he will take to it?'

'Like a fish to tartare sauce,' said Morgan.

'A crude analogy.'

'Ah well.' Morgan sounded bored like a man with no use for parts of speech. He and Pemberton were speaking from experience. They themselves had been present the other night – Phillips had been at the Literary Society, where a literary denizen had been expounding his 'secrets of success' with a somewhat puzzled air that was mistakenly construed as modesty (for he was as much mystified as the public were impressed by the critics' acclaim) – when Gifford had been beaten for doing his Extra Work in the rears after Lights Out. They had been present and so now spoke from experience. Pemberton explained that Phillips's presence was requested in the Library at 9.05 p.m. precisely, for summary judgement was to be executed that night.

'On a pal o' yourn, oi believe,' added Morgan.

'Any friend of Phillips's is a friend of Phillips's.'

'They're just good friends. Any rumours to the contrary are sedulously – put about.'

'C'est la vie.'

'Ooh là là !'

But then a change came over the place. Phillips saw Pemberton catch Morgan's hooded eye and smile.

'Feeding time,' said Pemberton, and stepping forward and opening the bird-cage, he dangled the caterpillar at the entrance. The bird hopped out greedily, chirruping with nervous anticipation. Pemberton dropped the caterpillar, which was still alive and which crawled off across the carpet quite placidly, as if wondering how best to adapt itself to its new surroundings, and took the body of the bird in his right hand and its head in his left. In a single movement he clenched his left fist, twisted his wrists in contrary directions, and flung the body of the hedge-sparrow back into the cage.

'That'll teach you to have oiks round to your room at night,' said Pemberton vindictively. But Morgan's dark face was like an African mask, expressionless, soulless, not particularly triumphant.

Scarfe had been in a state of shock ever since leaving the Bishop. He didn't feel like they do in the novels, not being the kind of person met with in the novels, 'as if the world had cracked about his ears,' but it had. All he felt was that nothing anyone did or said could ever concern him again. Let them live their own lives, just let them get on with it. So that the next morning at Early School he sat in his accustomed place with an abstracted air that was quite untypical of him. And even in Chapel – and the hymn 'For all the saints' was his especial favourite – he never opened his mouth, but stood, hymn book open at random in front of him, and let the tidal wave of sound surge over and submerge him. Only his finger and thumb were rubbing away at each other and his eyebrow was twitching. And then the whole congregation turned to face the East Window for the Creed, but he remained unmoved, on a different planet, the only adult at a Punch and Judy show. He didn't hate anyone or despise anyone, he was simply not interested this morning, thank you kindly, and, if his memories floated back disobediently twelve hours, he shook his head uncomprehendingly and shut out the memories. He remained quite static in Dynamics and in Chemistry his Bunsen burner consumed the oxygen unheeded. He ate little of the ham and salad at lunch and seemed hardly aware of the whispering of the gossips round him. And when someone, by tradition almost, ignored his request for the potatoes, Scarfe muttered: 'Have it your own way, then,' and sank back into lethargy.

That afternoon Berwick, the Captain of Games, was to organize a run to Locks and back, a distance of some six miles. Those members of the house whom Berwick, a particularly fine and objective judge of such things, regarded as 'slackers' were to participate and Berwick himself would accompany them. They were gruesome affairs these runs, because, as Berwick saw it, and he had a clear view unclouded by sensitivity, all men were born equal, at least with regard to turns of speed and staying power. It therefore followed that the flat-footed, the underdeveloped, the halt, the lame, and the blind (only in Manningham's there weren't any blind) were nothing so much as 'idle slackers' and 'lazy dogs' and should, if there were any real justice in the land, be flogged within an inch of their worthless lives. Or exposed on a mountain-side. Or hamstrung. So; those picked out for this particular run included – witness the notice-board – A. P. Scarfe, who, being at best 'typical yeoman stock' and at worst a 'malingering guttersnipe', could hardly be expected in any event to 'run like a gentleman'; and so must be taught.

'Look here, old boy,' said Berwick, wincing, 'I've put you down for the run this afternoon.' And the high-jump this evening, he thought to himself with satisfaction. 'Must keep up your training, you know, what with the harvest coming along.'

Scarfe didn't look up; didn't respond; didn't seem to be paying much attention really. His white slip of a tie was soiled, and the knot loose. On the back of his collar some joker had printed in red Biro: 'Kiss me.' His shoulders were flecked with dust or dandruff.

'Two-fifteen at the Boys' Entrance, then.'

Scarfe turned to him, like a man suddenly made aware, by tripping over the stumps, of a rather nasty, legless beggar in the streets.

'I shan't be there,' he said.

'You will, you lazy bugger—' began Berwick, but Scarfe had gone strolling off aimlessly, as if it was all over bar the communiqué. Berwick, understandably roused, followed him at once with a face like a diplomatic note, if not an ultimatum, but Scarfe had vanished into the rears, and locked the door. And, since diplomatists, even in this day and age, are unaccustomed to negotiate, or even threaten, through a locked lavatory door, there was nothing for it but for Berwick to retire to his room, mutter under his breath, and put on his shorts. This was the limit. God damn it, if you were told to run you ran, unless you were a . . . A what? Berwick snorted. He didn't have time to get metaphysical about it; if you were told to run you ran, God damn it, and if you didn't run you were beaten. That was the code of an Etonian and a gentleman. But Scarfe – unconstitutionally – was sulking.

And throughout the long afternoon, while Berwick was dragging the flat-feet and the bow-legs and the spindle-shanks and the weaklings after him, very often by the scrawny scruffs of their necks, while their skinny legs pumped away like the needles of sewing-machines, Scarfe remained sulking in the rears, reading over and over the faceless names etched on the walls. It was an afternoon

punctuated with desperate regularity by the dripping of
the water down the walls of the stand-ups, and the
occasional, threatening roar as the cistern filled and
refilled itself like some great sottish tosspot trying to get
itself drunk on bottled cyder.

Public School boys are not merely conservatives, they are
by nature totalitarian reactionaries. Nowhere else but in
the Public Schools does the spirit of the Drones Club and
Blandings Castle live on with such loyal enthusiasm;
nowhere else may such embryo fogeyism or blimpishness
pass quite unquestioned. Nowhere else is Socialism, that
'attempted corner in ideas', treated with such lofty
disdain; and yet nowhere is an oligarchy of such uncom-
promising severity accepted without demur. Totalitarian
reaction! And, if they cannot have it both ways, they
would generally plunk for totalitarianism. They live in a
régime that is by constitution and by popular rumour a
free one, certainly freer at Eton than at many other
schools, yet they subjugate themselves to a society in which
in practice they have neither freedom of will, freedom of
choice, nor freedom of action. They would never question
this. To give one relevant example; it is remarkable that
the existing rights of appeal against summary corporal
punishment (to the housemaster, to the Headmaster and,
by fanciful but untested tradition, to the President of Pop)
remain virtually uninvoked. In fact they live a life of utter
subservience to – well, to an ideology, and what is more
remarkable very few of them think or talk of politics at all.
   Phillips was considering this, insofar as his limited
experience and subjectivity allowed him to consider it, as
he dug a grave for the hedge-sparrow in his window-box.
He knew that Scarfe was to be punished and he suspected
that the punishment would be severe, and he believed that
Scarfe deserved his punishment, but just for a moment –

in a revolutionary mood, no doubt, as he buried an innocent martyr – he wondered, was it Christian, no, was it fair to punish him? Because mingled with the Etonian's belief in 'taking your punishment' was the Englishman's obstinate and instinctive sympathy with the underdog. And, if ever there was an underdog . . . Phillips's doubting was abortive, but he was left with a curiosity, no more, as to how Scarfe would take it. After all, the rules had been formed for Etonian sons of Etonian sons of Etonians, not for – well, nobodies from East Anglia. As Defries, who had been round on a fact-finding mission earlier in the day, had put it:

'It will be in the nature of an experiment, won't it? And, after all, that's what guinea-pigs are for, isn't it, my dear chap?'

CHAPTER SIX

SCARFE knew that he was for it, Good, Hard and Proper. But Good, Hard and Proper presented no terrors for him. He had been beaten before on two occasions, and neither time had he absolutely ruined himself by breaking down in front of them, which, of course, was what they wanted. But there was this difference between then and now. Then he had had a clear conscience and had therefore retained his pride, for they were silly, probably trumped-up, vindictive charges, which would not have fooled anyone. On those occasions he had cried with anger afterwards, but at the time there had been nothing to it. It had been like a game of forfeits; he had just been the unlucky one, that was all, and it was not much worse than in the old days when he had been first out in those horrible musical games and had had to stand in front of them all and recite 'Mary had a . . .' or 'Polly put the . . .' as a forfeit. Oh it had hurt him all right, but not his dignity, not his spirit.

'They can't kill me,' he had told himself, 'they can't *kill* me,' and he had retained his pride.

But this time he was muddled. Had he really been in the wrong to call on Tom like that? He had only wanted to win him over (only?), but it was quite clear in the rules about visiting people after prayers; and if they had found out about his moonlight saunter to the Bishop, then he would be lucky if he got away with Good, Hard and Proper. Not that he cared very much. And by ordinary standards there was no excuse for shirking a run; that alone would have been plenty. He tried the old formula: 'They can't *kill* me,' but to his surprise found that he didn't much care if they did. There was one ordinary

precaution that he might as well take; he would be a fool
not to try, but he had better be quick because the bell for
prayers might go at any moment. Scarfe unhitched his
braces and lowered his trousers, wetted a flannel in the
wash-basin and folded it in, quite flat, so that it wouldn't
show through, next to his bare behind. Then pulling on
his trousers and fastening them, he put his mirror at an
angle on the floor, bent over, and looked through his legs
to see if the flannel could be seen. No. They couldn't catch
him out that way. That was fine because, so they told him,
a wet flannel was the best, the very best, the real Fortnum
and Mason's of padding, whatever Fortnum and Mason's
was. (One or two reactionaries, however, swore by
blotting-paper.) Just a minute, though; there was something else . . . Taking a stick (an old chair leg) in his right
hand and pivoting on his hips he smote himself – a little
clumsily – on the bottom. There was a damp sort of noise.
Blast it, blast it, blast it! Good, Hard and Proper. Working
now with an urgency near to panic, he once again
lowered his trousers, removed the flannel, rubbed himself
comfortable with a towel, and began to pack handkerchiefs
into his underpants. Nobody swore by handkerchiefs, but
surely they must be better than nothing. In the middle of
this frantic operation, the Prayer Bell started ringing. A
stupid, urgent, *stupid* noise. Once again fiddling with the
buttons of the braces and the flies, he threw open the door
and hared down the passage. He could feel the handkerchiefs slipping. A trail of them, like the spoor of an animal,
followed him down the corridor. He charged back and
retrieved them (unlike an animal), then once more made
for the Pupil-Room, where the prayers were held.
(Morgan: 'Manningham believes in holding prayers in
P-hole – i.e. Pupil Room – because there he asserts his
authority and can keep an eye on God.' This was unfair of
Morgan; Manningham shut his eyes when he prayed,

4*

knowing all the usual prayers by heart.) He arrived in the middle of 'We have left undone those things which we ought to have done . . .' and when Manningham, standing at the tall, puritanical reading-desk, raised his eyes from his cupped hands – stars behind bars – he deliberately stopped the prayer, requiring God to wait tense with anticipation, and then coughed and resumed with a more emphatic intonation: '. . . And have done those things which we ought not to have done, and there is no health in us . . .'

Scarfe's bottom was still a bit damp, which set his teeth on edge with childhood memories, perhaps, of rubber sheets, and his pockets were stuffed with clean, crumpled handkerchiefs, and for the first time that day he suddenly felt utterly afraid. The fear seemed to strike at his stomach and then leap like flames to the throat and the bowels. His hands were even trembling. Opening his mind, he said under his breath: 'Don't let them beat me, oh God, don't let them hurt me,' but then realized that he could expect no help from that direction. He had denied Him in dirty whispers, dry and dirty, in the rears, and now that he needed Him, it was too goddamn late. The irony of it, as they say, was painful.

It is one way of looking at things to suggest that unless there is only one person in a room, there are always two people in a room. That sounds unremarkable, almost silly. But if there are three or more people in a room, two of those will be as it were elasticated together by a mutual something. That sounds vague and silly. Two will always be impressing, impinging on, attracting to, each other. Two will always be 'glossy'.

In four chairs in a semi-circle facing the door sat Morgan, Pemberton, Phillips and Berwick. They were ostensibly reading magazines. In actuality they were waiting. Standing to one side was Defries, waving his cane like a cavalry general his sword. Every now and then he brought it down heavily on the arm of one of the battered old Library chairs and bits of stuffing would rise suddenly and then sink again lazily, free-falling, by their own volition, too casually, surely, for any gravitational forces. Once again Tschaikovsky thundered from the radiogram. The pin-ups, shot full of holes like early Christian martyrs, looked down coyly from the walls. Phillips and Defries were glossy.

Outside the door Scarfe stood and trembled. The fear was still with him. He was unpadded. 'You are wanted by the Library. Will you go along and wait outside.' Phillips as junior member had come along, knocked on the door and said that, the rigmarole by rote, and added nothing, dropped nothing. Even the cry of 'Tom——!' which rever- berated after him like the scream of a gull, but more of a whine, didn't even cause him to break his step. And Scarfe had left the flannel and the handkerchiefs in his room, and some blotting-paper which he had forgotten about, and come straight down, always hugging the walls, as if he were afraid of thunderbolts.

Time, as you must expect, passed. Tschaikovsky scratched to silence and through the panels of the door, one of which was splintered, echoed Defries's: 'Come in.'

As Scarfe more or less strode through the door, though naturally he wasn't fooling anybody, Phillips stole a glance at him and ducked down behind *Esquire*. Phillips's no more than curious eyes gave place to the bulging lecherous ones of the *Esquire* Man himself in a grotesque transforma- tion. Phillips and Scarfe were glossy. Defries now, in spite of the cavalry general façade, counted for less than nothing. The shine was off him. However, he began to strut and prance in the way that an angry little man does, and work himself into a lather. Morgan, Pemberton and

Berwick behind their magazines turned over a page from time to time to keep up the pretence, but watched Scarfe and waited.

'You realize, of course,' Defries stormed, rather ridiculously because he had started off in an uncomfortably high key and couldn't modulate without lack of authority, 'that you could quite well have been expelled for being in Phillips's room last night. There are no mitigating circumstances. You had not even been invited,' a subtle touch of bitter irony there to entrench the point deeper, 'and you have no excuse to offer.'

'I—' said Scarfe.

'It would be culpable in me to deal leniently with you for this offence alone, but that is not all. I hear from Berwick here that you deliberately flouted his orders this afternoon and shirked a training run. Now you may not have had the same advantages at home as some of us; it would be charitable to assume that your environment is at fault. However, in a matter as serious as this in which your imprudent lust—' Blast, he had got carried away! He hadn't meant to say that. After all, when you *looked* at him, or, for that matter, *listened* to him – 'your criminal folly, your blind disobedience to the rules, your non-co-operation with authority, your filthy appearance and behaviour, all combine to render you despicable in the extreme, I have no alternative but to beat you as you have never been beaten before.' A significant pause. 'And let me say that you are incredibly lucky to get away with it without being sacked. Moreover, there is no one in this room who thinks any more of you than that' (a click of the fingers) 'or who would give twopence for your chances of remaining in the school another month. Now, have you anything to say before I beat you?'

'No . . . that is . . . I . . .' Scarfe's voice failed him. Why was he prolonging the agony? His unfortunate head seemed to be balanced on its thin column and held up-right by invisible wires, and it was as if at any moment it might loll over and crack those thin bones that tightened the skin on his neck. 'No, nothing.'

But there was still not the slightest bit of gloss on Defries. Phillips sat there reading over and over a sentence about 'the extraordinary reputation of the English Stilton Cheese', anything, anything not to catch Scarfe's eye, not to be moved by the pathos in his very stance. No, he deserved to be beaten, if only for his stupidity and his whining. All that talk about conversion. Why didn't he just mind his own business? With the utmost ferocity Defries bent the cane into a menacing parabola and snapped:

'Now get out, and wait outside until I call for you.'

A *Tatler*, a *Queen*, an *Esquire*, and a *Man Junior*, not all that inappropriately representing those behind them, were lowered, and the *Tatler* was the first to speak.

'Very definitive, Defries, I thought,' said Pemberton, 'the ultimate in razzes.'

'Come on, give me a hand with the flipping table,' said Berwick.

While Morgan put on once again the start of the Tschaikovsky, the table was brought out into the centre of the room, and the flap raised. Defries again was testing the cane on the arm of the chair.

'Nine, I think,' he said. Phillips drew in his breath. Nine was the traditional maximum, although in the bad days of Primrose twelve had been commonplace, or had sadistic time aggravated the punishment? And nine, with a Sixth-form or a Pop cane, was plenty. Berwick rounded on Phillips suspiciously.

'Any objection?' he asked.

'No objection,' said Phillips.

'Looking forward to it?' asked Pemberton.

Phillips stiffened. Now was the time to register his protest.

'Haven't looked forward to anything so much for years,' he said sarcastically. It was a feeble protest.

'Why, my dear chap, don't you think nine is the right number?' Defries sounded as if he genuinely wanted to know.

'Oh yes. Yes, quite right.'

Morgan crowed like a cock, and Pemberton almost burst something laughing.

Mrs. Molarkey had been at Eton three and a half weeks and had made her mark, although it was more of a dent really. Her room had become by turns a Star Chamber, a confessional, a larder, an operating theatre, a store-room, a council-chamber, a home. Instructed by the Dame that she was to call 'all the young gentlemen Mr. This or Mr. That whatever their rank', she had preferred to be less formal and more possessive by addressing them all 'mai dear' or 'mai lamb'. The young ones flocked round her, jockeying for position like little fish with a whale, and she told them stories. About 'mai late lamented father who was a detective at Scotland Yard' or 'his father who was a Diplomatist with a pungent for hia living'. Like all the best stories they had more regard for probability than truth. If they were bullied she restored their self-respect with understanding and chocolate fudge; they felt too old for that kind of sympathy, but they took it and chewed it and liked her the more for it. With the older ones she became gruff and less sentimental, and put away her fudge, but if they tried anything on her, or if she caught them at anything, then they would be admonished:

'Ai wonder whether your deah mother would be proud if she was to see you now,' and, sure enough, they would look sheepish and rage inwardly and excoriate her (quite

a job) afterwards with their friends. 'That silly old busy-
body', 'that great pregnant bitch', they would murmur, but
never in her hearing. They were too well-mannered for that.

As Mrs. Molarkey shambled back to her room she saw
Scarfe standing outside as white as a psychic researcher.
He was flat against the wall and his head was lolling to
one side. Mrs. Molarkey liked Scarfe but was unable to
classify him. She knew he was different from the 'young
gentlemen', but how it had happened, or why, she couldn't
hazard. How she knew he was different was because of his
voice and because he slept in his socks, but what that
added up to, well it was anyone's guess.

'Whai, what's the metter?' she asked him, and made to
touch his forehead, but he shrank away from her without
saying a word, so she added: 'Ai'm excess beggage, em
Ai?' trying to raise a smile, and then went into her room
with a shrug of her monumental shoulders, like a coal-
heaver emptying his sack. There was a concert on the
Home and then a programme about the trials of an
unmarried mother whose child was born deaf and dumb,
so she settled herself prodigiously into her chair, broke
wind a couple of times with refined abandon, and switched
on her Ultra.

'. . . Presto, Andante and Allegretto . . .' said a beautiful
voice, and Mrs. Molarkey's face creased into placid good-
humour as the music started. A few minutes later her
knitting (socks for soldiers at the front; it was a pattern
she had grown accustomed to) hopped from her capacious
lap as a muffled swish and a thud from the opposite side of
the corridor startled her into alertness. And she knew
now, having heard all the talk on the morning after
Gifford's beating up – although she had said that she
didn't believe the half of it – at once what it must be. But
it must not be. She recollected the lolling head of that poor
frightened lamb and her duty became clear.

Like a volcanic island rising from the surface of the sea, Mrs. Molarkey and her embonpoint rose simultaneously from the chair. Then with stately alacrity she charged through the door and into the corridor. Swish . . . thud! More distinctly this time. Pushing open the Library door, Mrs. Molarkey drew herself to her full width, puffed out her cheeks in outrage, seized Defries's cane in mid-descent, and broke it contemptuously across her knee. There was a moment's silence during which a myth was born.

Scarfe was bent double with the back of his neck pressed against the flap of the table. She nudged him with her elbow. And, overcome by emotion, years of severely repressed motherhood and the urgency of the situation, she cried to Scarfe:

'Get the 'ell out of 'ere, ducks!' And then, tossing her head at Defries like a wounded horse, she added:

'And if you want to use this bloody thing on me, come and bloody get me!'

'I'm very sorry, Mrs. Molarkey,' Manningham said some time later, with the weariness in his voice of a man whom the world is too much with, 'just as you were settling in so nicely, but interference in the internal affairs of the house just cannot be tolerated. You do understand that, don't you?'

Mrs. Molarkey wrapped herself in her dignity, and looked out of the windows of her soul at him in scorn:

'Ai understand,' she said, more refined than ever after that unforgivable lapse, 'only too well that they was maltreating that unfortunate lamb, and Ai will not sit bai and let them do that.'

'Yes, Mrs. Molarkey, I think I can appreciate your motives in the affair, however misguided. But I fear you can hardly expect us to alter a system perfected by five hundred years of practice just because your sensibility has been offended. The Public School system is bigger than both of us, Mrs. Molarkey, so I think quite the best thing would be for you to pack your bags and leave in the morning; you may, of course, collect a month's wages from the Dame, and, so far as references are concerned, you may rely on me to bear in mind the extreme delicacy of your nature.'

'Ai shall be very happy to leave in the morning. Ai shall not be requairing references. Nor have Ai any wish to prolong mai stay in a houseful of Nazis. And, as for your "young gentlemen", Ai have seen truer gentlemen cleaning out lavatories in the Cromwell Road.'

'I'm sure you have,' said Manningham.

'Come, Hesta,' said Mrs. Molarkey to her niece.

But Hesta remained rooted to the spot. Her little hands quivering like moths' wings with some great mental turmoil, she blanched and blushed and blanched again. Then, drawing in her cheeks, she cried out in a tremulous coloratura: 'Nazis!' and turned on her heel and left the study.

Scarfe was very surprised after the first two strokes of the cane to feel nothing but a nudge in the ribs. It was such an anti-climax that he almost cried out with the very unexpectedness of it. His whole body had been tense, his breath indrawn, his black-rimmed fingernails cutting into the sweaty palms of his hands. But when Mrs. Molarkey nudged him and a whiff of Mrs. Molarkey, compounded of talcum, frying-fat and Mrs. Molarkey, came to his nostrils, he stiffened for a split second, and then relaxed and stood up with a puzzled, almost aggrieved expression on his face. He seemed at first not to have understood what she had said, but suddenly he darted for the door and was gone. Gratefully. Because anyone who's ever been beaten will tell you that the first two really don't count – unless they happen to fall on precisely the same spot; and it is not until the third or fourth when the stripes begin to criss-cross that the real pain begins. Scarfe scampered to his room and examined the damage in the mirror, and the skin was not even broken. That was nothing, and waves of relief flooded his whole body. Huh, that would show them, and he didn't think they would try again. Too much of a loss of face and far too embarrassing for that stupid old Defries with his 'beat you as you've never been beaten before'. He laughed aloud and remembered that God had answered his prayer, in spite of his blasphemies, and sent a guardian angel in the shape of . . . It was too funny, and he laughed again, rocking himself to and fro on the bed and stuffing the pillow into his mouth, while the tears poured down his cheeks. But he was not hysterical, just overwrought. Half undressed, half in and half out of bed, half laughing, half crying, his faith half-restored and his soul half-healed, he lay there until he became tranquil and then quite happily and cheerfully undressed – except for his socks – and climbed into his raggled bed and fell asleep.

Defries, however, was finding it awfully difficult to sleep. To be interrupted in the middle of a beating-up session is as frustrating as to be interrupted in the middle of – well, anything, and he was all a-tingle. Of one thing, though, he was certain. Scarfe would not escape that easily. Oh, no. Just because of an unpredictable, mad, old lady, just because of Manningham's domestic problems, crime should not be allowed to go unpunished, not while he was Captain. He had a responsibility and a position and specific instructions not to be lenient. All right then, he would cut down that green bay tree even if he had to hack and hack and hack at it. He would have to go down to the Court Hairdressers first thing in the morning and buy another cane. Out of the fine money presumably.

And it was no earthly use sending a fag down to collect it, because it would be sabotaged, sure as eggs . . . A horse-hair inserted, they used to say, so long as you knew where and how to make the insertion, would do the trick. And then, since it wouldn't do to be seen carrying a cane, because then everyone would start asking questions (not that he had anything to hide), he would have to put it down a trouser-leg and bring it back that way.

As you would expect Scarfe had behaved badly again that night. Anyone but a stinking oik would have told Mrs. Molarkey where she got off and stayed on and taken the rest of his beating like a man. With a broken cane? Well, no doubt if Scarfe had had enough guts to stay on and take what was due to him, he, Defries, would have let him off the rest. He wasn't a brute beast. But if Scarfe went scurrying off like that . . . Well, no doubt if you were a guinea-pig you had a false sense of values, but, since he, Defries, had taken on the responsibility of setting Scarfe on the right path, then he would not shirk that responsibility. It was a duty he would even relish.

But, Jesus, it was no use trying to sleep in this frame of mind. His nerves were shot, and it was all the fault of that . . . Defries realized that there was only one thing to do if he was to get that oik out of his mind and get some sleep. And, while the moonlight streamed into his room coolly and limpidly, and moths and may-bugs slapped against his pillow, he did it.

CHAPTER SEVEN

PHILLIPS had invited Jill, the girl in the yellow dress, to Eton for the Fourth of June. His parents would not be there, as they were holidaying in Majorca, where they had a villa 'on the North uninhabited side', and so he felt free to invite her.

Dear Tom, she wrote,

Thank you so very much for inviting me to your June the 4th. All the girls here are terribly jealous of me, and Mrs. Foster didn't want me to go, but couldn't stop me as I haven't had my weekend off this term. By the way is it all right if I bring my brother along? You remember him, he was on the boat. You see, it's his car, and otherwise I don't see how I could get to Eton. He's really very nice and if his sister likes him, everyone must! – Phillips couldn't subscribe to that – *I think that the weather is frightful, and I am thoroughly fed up to the brim. If it doesn't clear up by the 4th I shall certainly have something to say. (However pleasant company can always relieve the depression!!!) I am using an awful amount of paper, I am trying to finish this pad so that I can buy another one. It also makes the letter seem longer. I am afraid that this is all the news, except that we have another dance with the Nautical College next term. I do look forward to seeing you again, really I do. Watch your boathook.*

Love,

Jill XXXX.

P.S. When are you going to send me a photograph?

He read this first at Tuesday breakfast, sitting at the top table now, where they were less inquisitive, and he read it again in Chapel, camouflaged behind the Eton

College Hymn Book, and he read it again during history, while Garibaldi roused the peasants. But, try as he might, it was hard to read very much into it. Her brother would be there and that just about put paid to it all, didn't it? And who cared about the Nautical College? But then, by a conscious effort of will, he was able to recapture something of the tenderness he had felt after their midnight swim, and wrote Jill a letter full of 'darlings' and 'longings'. Really that kind of letter practically wrote itself, providing you put it straight in the envelope and sent it off without re-reading it. And without actually committing yourself. That, Phillips decided, was the secret of love-letter-writing.

As a matter of fact the arrival of Jill's letter was quite a blessing, however many brothers she had. Because he just didn't feel keen to spend too much time thinking about last night. No one had appeared in a particularly favourable light, except possibly for Mrs. M., and she was gone already, so rumour had it. And he was unable to disguise from himself the fact that he had been troubled by her intervention almost as much as Defries had been. His curiosity had been certainly aroused, and he had found it increasingly difficult to keep up the pretence of reading his magazine. And when the beating had started he had found himself pressing his knees together in his excitement. He supposed it was like in the jungle when the victory of the strong (Defries) and the beautiful (the curve of the cane) over the weak and the ugly was always exhilarating, and when the rest of the pack tore the injured member to pieces. He was sure that they had all hoped, as he had, that Scarfe would cry out.

So he felt all the more uncomfortable when Pemberton drew him aside after boys' dinner and told him:

'You know we're going to complete the good work tonight, don't you? There won't be any boys' maid to

interrupt this time, but there may possibly be a boy
unmade, don't you think?'

The procedure was much the same as the previous night
but shorter and altogether less formal. Four chords of
Tschaikovsky were the total ration and the furniture
removers did their stuff before Scarfe was summoned.
Then Defries said:

'Good evening, Scarfe, I hope I find you penitent?'
Scarfe said nothing. He just looked pale and drawn and
rather foolish. He was, inevitably, missing a cuff-link, and
his shirt-sleeve flapped about his arm like a flag of sur-
render. 'Well, of course, you have the advantage of us
there, Scarfe; if you don't choose to pass the time of day
with us, we can't make you, can we? We can only teach
you manners if you're willing to learn from us. Are you
willing to learn from us, Scarfe? We do feel, my dear chap,
that you're in need of instruction.'

'I wish . . . I wish that you would get it over with,' said
Scarfe.

Defries smiled. 'What a gift for over-simplification you
do have! Well, you see, if you had not acted as you did
last night and left us so rudely, it would have been over
long since. Ah well, as you wish then. You had better get
your head under the table, Scarfe.'

Defries's cold sarcasm was far more venomous than his
hot anger had been. He was relaxed tonight, sure of himself, and, as he spoke, his glittering little eyes were fixed
on the other's sulky brown ones, and his head was weaving
back and forth in a most discomfiting way. Phillips
almost found the spectacle repulsive, but he wouldn't have
been elsewhere. Scarfe bent down and the pin-stripe
trousers were stretched over his broad buttocks. With the
light full on it the material looked very shiny.

'Tighter,' said Defries, 'if you would be so kind.'

Through his legs Scarfe could see the grinning figure of Defries, brandishing the bamboo, and *upside-down*, as he came rushing in with his arm upraised. This time as the new cane cut into the old bruises the very first stroke burnt him like fire. Defries was taking his time. Scarfe, anything so as not to think of the pain, closed his eyes and counted five before the cane struck him again. His teeth bit into his lip, his nails into his hand, and his toes curled into the floor, as he struggled for support against the assault. After the fourth stroke he whimpered, and after the fifth, in an extraordinary, surprised way he called out: 'Ouch!' After the sixth he cried: 'No!' and as the seventh came in he lost his nerve and straightened up to put off, even momentarily, the agony of impact. He could feel himself sweating all over. After the eighth he collapsed on the floor and refused to move even when Defries prodded him with his toe.

'I haven't finished yet,' Defries spat out between his teeth, 'get up and be a man. *I haven't finished yet.*'

Only one thing mattered to Scarfe, which was that they shouldn't see his tears. He put his hands to his face, stood up slowly, swaying a little, and then made a dash for the door. He missed the door handle and fumbled and Defries was just about to go after him when Morgan said quite quietly: 'No, don't' and put out a restraining arm. The sound of Scarfe's feet echoed down the hollow corridor and Defries asked:

'Why did you do that?'

'Vell, ve 'ave vonce more unteruppted been, nicht wahr? 'E vill 'ave vonce more to com ze full treatment for, nicht wahr? Zair iss lodds of time, nicht wahr?'

'Tomorrow . . .' said Defries thoughtfully. Morgan nodded. Berwick was grinning at full stretch and Pemberton lay back with his eyes closed, for all the world like a bank-clerk sun-bathing on the beach. He was breathing deeply. Phillips said nothing and turned the pages of a magazine, but quickly, much too quickly. Something had happened to him, and he was appalled.

The Honourable Alethea Berwick turned her big, beautiful eyes upon those of her dressmaker. He had big, beautiful eyes too.

'My God, darling,' she said, 'my darling God, how can you be so tedious?'

'But it's for your own sake, madame, or rather for the sake of that son of yours.'

'But honey, he's not a minor. He's got hair on his chest now.'

'Hair on his chest!' The young man with a mouthful of pins made a moue.

'Dark and crinkly,' said Alethea. 'Why is it?' she asked a rather sour-looking Modigliani on the wall, 'why is it that the hair on the chest is the first to go grey?' Modigliani said nothing, but the young dressmaker sighed and twisted his love-curl round a finger. 'But the heart, my dear madame, the heart grows old,' he lyricized meaninglessly.

'That's a lot of crap!' Alethea said with superb disdain. 'The heart is the one thing which doesn't. I'm thirty-seven' – the two of them did swift calculations in their heads and came up smiling – 'but when I see the light and shade of – well – of one of your beautiful creations, my bird of paradise, or a pretty little sailor all spruced up and shining in his nice, blue suit, then for a moment anyway I too am truly young.'

'Hold still, madame, *please*.'

'Not in *entire* forgetfulness and not in *utter* nakedness . . .' Alethea went on, à propos of what the young man would never know, 'but trailing clouds of glory . . . Do you trail clouds of glory, my own?' She lowered her bristling eyelashes and shuddered hopefully, as he made some trifling adjustment to the hem.

'That would be telling, madame,' mysteriously answered her own.

'Shades of the prison-house begin to close upon the growing boy,' continued Alethea, muffling him playfully in her petticoat, 'which brings us back to that son of ours.'

'Of yours, madame. I wasn't born. Remember?'

Alethea pouted, as well she might. 'How can I remember your not being born? Of ours. Of *ours*,' she went on reminiscently, 'poor old Alfred! The sweetest little sonofa – stockbroker you ever saw. He was the *prettiest* thing when he twirled his little umbrella!'

'Yes, well, I don't think I could allow my sister possibly . . .'

'. . . but on the fourth of June . . .'

'. . . to take part in such a shady . . .'

'. . . and he's such a steady and sweet-tempered boy . . .'

'. . . a well brought-up girl, with feelings . . .'

'. . . and, after all, she's only a milliner . . .'

'. . . and what do I get out of it, madame?' They were both silent for a moment.

'It all depends on what you put into it, honey lamb,' answered Alethea, gaily ruffling his golden hair, 'but if it's currency you're after . . .'

'Oh, you're a terrible woman,' cried the young dressmaker, secretly delighted and undulating under her caress.

'How dare you speak to me like that!' suddenly snapped Alethea, arching her back, 'how dare you, you *tradesman*.' And she opened her hand and brought it hard across his face. 'Keep your horrid little trollope of a sister.'

'As madame wishes;' coldly and smarting.

Madame considered. Then at last: 'You know what madame wishes,' and took him off to clinch the deal.

Scarfe had gone to bed early and was fast asleep on

Wednesday evening when Phillips came to summon him once more to the Library. Scarfe had, in fact, asked the Dame's permission to miss prayers, and she, whose job was to minister to the body and let the devil take the soul, but who was more inclined to minister to the soul and let the mysterious functions of the body go to the devil, on this occasion made no objection. She did, however, remark his peakiness, and inquired if he felt quite well besides being tired, to which he replied that he felt fine. Was he keeping regular? Yes (blushing), he was keeping regular. The Dame believed that, so long as the boys' excretions were normal, their diet must be perfectly adequate, and so, being in charge of both intake and outlet, she was able to effect kitchen economies for her housemasters with a clear medical conscience. In any case the boys were not too conscientious themselves to judge by the 'epidemic' which suddenly erupted every half on the eve of the Corps field day. On such occasions she was inclined to decorticate them with: 'That is not what is meant by dying for your country!' while they, cursed once more with a lease of life, would flip their fingers at her behind her back.

'Wake up! You are wanted by the Library. Put a dressing-gown on, and go along and wait outside.' Phillips was able to make a quick getaway.

Drunk with sleepiness, Scarfe staggered out of bed, quite anaesthetized really, and along the corridor. What did it matter, their waking him? He could have found his way there, asleep; in a nightmare.

The pain this time was so acute that there was only one way to bear it. He imagined himself lying curled up on a vivid patch of moss by the side of a pool in a green forest. All around there was peace, absolute peace and quiet, and all he had to do was just to lie there. It was difficult to keep this picture in front of him with all the time this intolerable pain searing his buttocks, but he kept his eyes tight shut, and his mind at peace in the forest. After the fourth stroke the reopened wounds began to bleed, and the hot blood trickled down the backs of his legs. After the sixth stroke the forest vanished and he cried out in pain. He did not believe that he could have suffered the seventh and the eighth and the ninth stroke was the hardest of all. Phillips, watching, now almost screamed himself, but there was still that in him which cried out for the punishment to continue. More, more! Harder, harder! As for Defries, it was quite obvious that he had lost all control of himself. After the ninth stroke, Scarfe twisted round, his face contorted, and the expression on that face, the sleepiness in the eyes melted into tears, was remembered by everyone in that room for a long time afterwards.

Later, when Scarfe lay on his bed and sobbed and sobbed as if his heart would break, he was crying for the ruin of his body which he seemed to see now as something quite apart from himself, an innocent scapegoat. And pity, not self-pity, but pity for this ugly, laughable body of his, racked him as he sobbed. He lay in the dark so that he would not have to look at the mess they had made of him, and it was unfortunate he did so, because, if his light had been on, Manningham would not have passed his door as he went on his rounds. The housemaster would have liked to talk to the guinea-pig about his escapade; what had he really done it for – you can tell me, you know; and also he was curious to see if he had taken his punishment like a man. It hadn't been very manly to run out of the room like that the night before after just a couple of strokes, at least not the way Defries had described it to him, but then you never could tell with these grammar school boys. Other housemasters told him they were rather inclined to be soft, but Manningham thought it was unwise to generalize in matters of this kind.

Tuesdays, Thursdays and Saturdays are half-holidays at
Eton, and for 'Slack-Bobs', those who have attained a
responsible position in the school and have elected neither
to play cricket nor to row, the time between dinner and
'Absence', or Roll-call, at a quarter to six, is their own. A
few play golf at Datchet or, if especially privileged, at
Stoke Poges, and a few play tennis alongside the school
laundry, but Phillips, unless he was golfing, generally
went for long walks along the Thames. This Thursday, the
second day in June, the clouds were ragged and torn along
the seams, there was just an occasional flurry of rain, and
the dark, opaque river-water was piling up around the
struts of Windsor Bridge. The castle was at its most
impregnable, and its brutal outlines reared up into the
low, fleeting clouds, as if symbolizing man's one victory
over the elements. But, of course, symbols are in the eye
of the beholder. The occasional squares of light in the
windows (it was dark enough for that) added an ironical
touch of humanity.

Phillips turned right over the bridge, away from the
castle, and, keeping always close to the river, walked
towards Dorney Lock. He was in 'half-change', that is to
say, over his Eton trousers he had on a brown tweed
jacket and on his head the white and light blue 'scugger'
of the undistinguished athlete. He walked violently and
viciously, his knees forgotten, lifting his face to the rain
flurries until his cheeks were red and his eyes shining. Now
that it was all over he felt a disgust with the lot of them
and with himself, yet it was not a grand passion; he just felt
angry that he had been mixed up in such a sordid little
incident. He should have disassociated himself; he should
have abstained; he should have known nothing about it.
Scarfe was to blame, of course, and had been punished,
more harshly than was necessary perhaps, but others had
suffered similarly before and would again. He felt no sense

of injustice, would just rather not have been there, that was all. He could now even laugh to himself at the clumsy, pathetic defencelessness of Scarfe, but then suddenly, against a disturbed row of elms on the horizon, he saw, superimposed, that anguished face, when the ugliness was at once no longer funny.

He stopped walking and sat down abruptly on an oak bench. There was a plaque on it; the bench had been a gift to the Windsor Council from a mother whose youngest son had been drowned swimming in the Thames. To Phillips a bench seemed an inappropriate memorial, but he could not have explained why.

He had not been there long watching a waterlogged Senior Service packet bobbing by, when a middle-aged woman in a grey hooded mackintosh came and sat down by his side. He pretended not to have seen her, but after a minute or so she leant forward, turned to him, and looked straight into his eyes. He remarked that she was wearing no make-up of any kind, and that her lips were dry and cracked. Smiling politely and clasping her hands in each other so that she seemed to have rows and rows of long, articulate fingers, she said:

'Do you know what Saint John said about Christ? He said that He was the Word of God made flesh. Now isn't that wonderful?' And she paused for acknowledgement. Phillips smiled briefly and inclined his head, as if to show that it certainly was wonderful, and that it was wonderful of her to have appreciated how wonderful it was and that it was wonderful of him to have appreciated how wonderful she was, but just now he had more important things to think about, okay?

'I myself have seen Jesus Christ face to face, you know. It was just after our dear Queen's marriage, and my beloved husband had passed over to the other side – isn't that a wonderful phrase, the other side? – and I was

sitting at home, wondering if I had the courage to open
the Good Book, when suddenly the whole room was filled
with gold light and, right under my picture of the Good
Shepherd, *He* appeared.' The expression on her face had
changed now, and it was almost as if she was filled with
gold light, her eyes had become so radiant. 'Do you know
what He said?'

'No,' said Phillips. He couldn't imagine.

' "Your husband is with me in the Communion of the
Saints, and sends his love to you." Isn't that wonderful?'
She looked searchingly into his eyes, almost hypnotizing
him into acquiescence.

'Yes, wonderful,' he said, and her expression relaxed
into benevolence.

'I expect you think I dreamt it all, don't you, but there
on my wall, in letters of fire, is branded . . .' Her voice
trailed off.

'What?' Phillips asked reluctantly.

'The representation of a shepherd's crook.' Her voice
became more matter-of-fact, like someone reading a
business letter aloud. 'And then He left me, but before He
went, He showed me the Communion of Saints, and the
evil messengers of Satan too. But my husband, He showed
me not. If only the leaders of the world,' she went on
without apparently drawing breath, 'could see what I
had seen, they might be powers for good in the land.
Hitler, for instance, another Wesley, if he hadn't hated
the Jews. And we need another Wesley. But what do you
do, my child?'

'I'm at school here, you know,' said Phillips.

'If only the youth of today could see what I have seen,'
she said, 'they would not do the things they have done,
but would hear the beautiful words of Saint John the
Divine when he said—'

'Look, I've really got to go now,' said Phillips making

an effort. Her cracked lips tightened and the sweetness of her face twisted into a grotesque rage.

'Oh, generation of serpents!' she cried out, 'How long, Oh Lord, how long!' With one hand she grabbed Phillips by the arm in an irresistible Grendel-grip, and with the other she pulled from the pocket of her mackintosh a packet of postcards. 'Take one, take one!' Phillips took one and put it into his inside pocket; then smiling and muttering 'must run' he broke from her and made off along the bank towards Windsor. As he ran he could just hear through the wind her voice, crying: 'Run, run all you like, you can't escape from—' something or other. As soon as he dared he glanced back over his shoulder, and there she stood, just as he had left her, with one hand outstretched, looking after him. A gust of wind was carrying her postcards across the river, but even as he turned, the gust was over, and they dipped and touched the angry surface of the water. From a distance she looked neither radiant nor fanatic, he decided, just rather lonely and pathetic, and he was sorry that he had been so brusque at the end. He turned from her and walked on, aware that she was watching him, but when he had passed some willows which obscured him, he took out the postcard and looked at it. On one side was printed a postcard form with the usual instructions: 'Stamp to be affixed here' and 'Address only to be written this side', while on the other there was reproduced in a yellow tint the woman's photograph. She was dressed in a military battledress with khaki beret, and her eyes were closed. Her right hand was outstretched towards a glittering crucifix, and the other held a dagger. There was no legend.

Well really, Phillips thought to himself, I *do* find them. First Scarfe with all his prayers and conversions and Christ knows what *she* wanted. And he was filled with anxiety that there existed so many people in the world who didn't know the rules, who would discuss anything with just anyone, without shame. Somebody ought to put them right. There were hardly enough conformists for conformity as it was and order must be preserved at any cost ... Such emotional people ... No wonder the Empire was crumbling ... Naked exhibitionists starving themselves ... Pshaw!

Phillips tore the postcard in half and let it fall into a Windsor Corporation litter bin.

The river streamed menacingly past Rafts and licked the lawn of the Old House Hotel.

CHAPTER EIGHT

DEFRIES looked up from a James Hadley Chase.

'Bigby.'

'Yes, Defries.'

'Do you enjoy fagging for me?'

'Yes and no.'

'You can be honest with me.'

'Then no.' Bigby was working away angelically at Defries's Corps boots.

'I'm very sorry to hear that.'

'You need not be; the fault is in me.'

'Would you enjoy it better if I were to pay you?'

'It wouldn't make any difference.'

'Yes, but would you like me to?'

Bigby for the first time looked curiously at his fag-master. He paused like a comedian timing a joke.

'My father is probably richer than yours. I don't know. Still, I'd keep the money.'

'I see. And Russell?'

'Russell likes to sock. He's rather greedy.'

'Do you think you *should* be paid?'

'No, it wouldn't be wise.'

'Yes, of course, people might talk. Well, Bigby, that's a risk one must always take. Do people talk much about you?'

'Do you need these boots for tomorrow's parade? Because, if so, I'll take them with me and work on them after prayers.'

'Boots? Oh yes, yes. What I mean to say is, do they bully you, or mob you up, or – or anything?'

'When I let them.'

'*When* you let them? Not if?'

'Oh, when or if, I don't see it matters which. Is that all for tonight, Defries?'

'Yes, I think so, Bigby. Only, Bigby—' the fag had his hand on the handle of the door – 'if you do have any problems, with extra work or – or anything, maybe I can help. Fag-masters can be friends too, you know.'

'I'm sure they can,' said Bigby, looking Defries straight in the eyes without blinking, 'it's a good system really, isn't it?'

And with that Bigby trotted off down the passage, licking the tips of his fingers and smoothing his hair; which was hardly necessary. It was a dark evening, dark and hot. There was a low-pitched monotonous vibration in the air, inevitable, intolerable. Two flies were dancing round the light in a slow, measured tempo. Every so often one would leap at the other and the two would wrap themselves up in a boisterous, indistinguishable bundle, like two Walt Disney dogs fighting tooth and claw, then break apart and resume their sedate gavotte. Defries lay on his back on his bed and observed them with interest. He wondered what they were playing at. Mating? debating? fighting? killing time? or just fulfilling their function as flies in an ineffably complex pattern of creation, in which everything had a purpose, and nothing a meaning? Whatever it was they seemed to be enjoying themselves up there, casting their shadows on the cracked white paint of the ceiling.

The cuts that Scarfe had received had had no chance to heal, and were beginning to look very nasty. There was quite a chance that they might fester unless they received treatment quickly; but what could he do? He could always pour some T.C.P. into the bath when he had a bath, but it wasn't his bath-night for two nights yet, and he had no wish to see the Dame on a subject so personal. In point of fact he had no wish to see anyone very much. People need sometimes to be alone – it is as basic a need as the need to be with somebody – to be free from interruptions of sympathy or congratulation; free to work out an individual fate in moments of peace; free to make decisions; free to accept reversals of fortune; free from social criticism; free from the fear of appearing foolish; free from mass-freedom; by themselves.

But it is possible to go too far to the other extreme, and Scarfe's new lust for solitude was becoming neurotic. It seemed so long since Phillips had offered to mess with him, a long month certainly, and the idea now of sharing his food with, or breaking his bread with anyone, anyone at all, filled him with a nervous disgust. And to think that he had run like a hunted man through the night *to* the Bishop . . . and it all stemmed from that night, really. During the last four days he had been more alone than during any number of East Anglian springs. And since he had cut himself off from God, although he had an uneasy suspicion that God could not be excommunicated quite so easily, and grown away from his family, with a little manuring by society to ensure that he grew strongly in this new direction, and been rejected by Phillips, first in words and more recently in silence, he could justifiably pride himself on being now utterly alone. Justifiably, but it was not a very healthy sort of pride. Pride should not be born of desperation, but Scarfe was proud, desperate and alone. He was also in considerable pain, and was quite unable to sit down without discomfort. A corny joke, but not very funny. That evening, thankful at least to be *kneeling* in prayer, Scarfe looked up from his hands during the collect and there was Phillips glaring at him with an unrelenting intensity. Scarfe felt like an ant being burnt to death under a magnifying glass in the sun. But he was unable to interpret that fierce expression. Was it hostility? apology? or was there some kind of explanation that

would make sense of the whole senseless mess? Or did it
mean – it could well mean – that he was to be beaten
again that night? Let them all hand it out, let Tom wield
the cane himself, he could take it; at least his poor
mortified body could. A little more. Only a little more.
No, no more. But what about St. Paul? He had taken it
who knows how many times, and he certainly wasn't an
Etonian, or even an Englishman for that matter, though
in a way you could call him a guinea-pig.

As soon as prayers were over, having failed to feel himself particularly alone with or without God, at least with
those burning eyes on him, Scarfe hobbled to his room,
and there shut the door, closed the curtains of the window,
lay on his bed and covered himself with a rug. It was very
hot in the dark, on the bed, and the pores of his skin were
prickling as if he were walking naked through a swarm of
fireflies. He dug his face into the nap of the rug and the
perspiration trickled into his eyes and stung them.
Although the curtains were drawn a strangely lurid light
flickered from time to time on the walls of his room. It
was summer lightning. It sparkled over the Round
Tower, and glowed luminously on the battlements of the
castle. Its reflection shimmered in the river, twinkled in
the distance behind the arches of the Slough–Windsor
railway line. And always in a silence that was more
mysterious and compelling than the loudest clap of
thunder. Scarfe pulled the rug more tightly around him
and strained his senses for the footsteps outside his door.
He could tell Phillips's footsteps by the flapping of the
loose sole. Unless he wore his other pair of shoes . . .
Nothing. There was nothing. Why were they hesitating
tonight? By this time yesterday, and the day before that,
and the day before that . . . Scampering footsteps came
and went in the passage; Phillips never scampered; it
could be Russell or one of the other fags trotting along for

his fifteen-minute bath. Yes, he could just hear the water running. Now from the street voices and laughter came wisping up like smoke, dissipating as they rose. They were surburban voices, broad and ugly and direct; there was no mouthing nor slurring the vowels, no irony or affectation in the laughter. They were bloody oiks like he was, but Scarfe covered his ears. And dozed.

He saw himself wading out through the sea, which was hot and thick as pitch and clung to his legs, towards a sandbank on which a speed-boat was moored. The boat was full of merry-makers, among whom he could distinguish Phillips and Defries and they were laughing (but not with the laughter from the street) and beckoning, and there was one seat in the boat for him between two laughing girls with peeling, sun-splashed shoulders, but they wouldn't wait for him much longer, and it was hard work pounding through this sticky sea. He looked behind him. Across the effluvious surf rose the immense battlements and minarets of what he knew to be a broiler-plant, and at its gate his father stood steadily smiling at him. Just as he reached the sandbank the boat shot off with a whirr of propellers and the passengers cried with one voice: 'Sorry, old chap.' And he stood quite alone on the sand, and the tacky, black water flooded in from the sea in a solid, hissing wall and he was drowning, up to his neck in it, up to his chin, up to his stinging eyes, and the boat swept round lazily in an easy curve and slanted in towards him, its prow sharp as a blade of grass, and all the passengers were leaning over, and smiling down at him, and shouting: 'Sorry, old chap.'

'Sorry, old chap.' It was Manningham at the door, tall, slim, at his ease, smiling down at him. Scarfe was covered in perspiration, and he had knotted the rug round and round his body. Lightning still flickered behind the curtains. The boy was pale and fevered, and his eyes narrowed as he endeavoured to focus them on Manningham. The pupils were as big as windmills. 'Didn't know you were asleep.'

'Yes, sir, yes. What do you want?'

'Are you all right, Scarfe?'

'Yes, sir, I'm fine. I was just asleep, that's all. I mean, I was just dreaming.'

God, Manningham thought, won't anybody tell me anything? And in a moment of realization, sun breaking through the clouds if you like, he saw where he had gone wrong. Forty-five boys, for whom he was responsible, some of them almost certainly had souls – and it was responsibility enough to care for a single soul – and he could hardly tell them apart. Facially at the most. And he didn't like them. Not only that, but the antipathy was mutual. God, God – and why did *He* have to crop up all of a sudden? – what had he achieved? And then the moment was gone, the clouds had blotted out the sun if you like; Manningham was himself again.

'Well, Scarfe, you don't look exactly in the pink of condition to me. You had better come with me and see the Dame.'

Scarfe protested with the greatest vehemence; it was nothing, it was indigestion, it was a chill, it was nothing, but when Manningham suggested that the Dame would come to Scarfe, Scarfe, to his amazement, found he was unable to make a move to stop it.

'Sir, sir,' he called, but Manningham had gone. He felt extraordinarily foolish, lying there, twined in his rug, fully clothed, but there was really nothing for it. It was ridiculous, but he was paralysed.

Mrs. Molarkey had drawn her month's wages in lieu of notice, had girt up her loins and buckled on her armour and packed up her niece, and returned to London. On

arrival, as a special treat, she took Hesta with her on a
Number Fifteen bus trip from Paddington to Aldgate,
where she believed there might be 'prospects from a
certain party'.

In the front on the top they sat, either side of the gangway, with a whole double-seat each (that really *was* a
treat for Hesta) and said nothing. All along Praed Street
and Edgware Road they sat there like statues of saints,
borne in procession, and Oxford Street and Regent Street
were prostrate before them. The niece, perhaps not fully
attuned to the dignity and significance of the occasion,
pointed excitedly to a dress in Richard Shops and was
about to pass a remark on the subject of halter-necks, but
her aunt silenced her with an enormous forearm upreared
like a mitre. The Haymarket, Trafalgar Square and the
Strand, with their theatres and fountains, advertised and
honoured them and it was a wonder that Fleet Street
didn't produce a souvenir edition. Flags were out in the
City Streets and lunchtime crowds had postponed their
sandwiches to cheer or sneer (as their politics or their
friends prompted them) at the visiting royalty; but the
sneerers and schnorrers seemed poor creatures beside the
loyalists and the chattering foreign students and the
tourists and the sun. For Mrs. Molarkey it seemed like a
welcome home. At Ludgate Circus she cleared her throat
momentously and in the shadow of St. Paul's she began
to speak, thoughtfully, choosing her words.

'Well, we're well shot of that lot, aren't we?' she said,
and the refainment was out of her voice, 'we don't owe
the likes of them nothing, and we can muddle along
without them. Definitely.' Smiling secretaries craned their
scrubbed necks out of windows along Cannon Street and
waved at them; they needed a warming up to be properly
hot for royalty. 'I mean there's something rotten about
them all, wouldn't you say, Hesta? They enjoy things

differently, if you see what I mean. They've got too many manners.'

'But Auntie . . .'

The flags in Fenchurch Street fluttered their approval, and at Aldgate a West Indian conductor gave Mrs. Molarkey a pink hand down the stairs. She bowed her head regally to him and dismounted.

'I have a feeling I can get a job,' she told Hesta, as they safaried into the A.B.C., 'as barmaid at the Dun Cow. That will make a nice change. Oh definitely.'

But Hesta only giggled and helped herself to a bun.

The Dame was at first predisposed to conclude that Scarfe was faking, and to diagnose a fraud, as if he were an undefended murderer struck dumb in the dock. But when she studied him more closely she understood that here was something outside her experience. In fact, in spite of her hereditary title, her hygienic outlook on life, and her readiness to find sickness in the mind of a boy on the paltry evidence of a rooted-out magazine or a vulgar drawing, she was quite unqualified as a nurse. However, she had kept the house acceptably healthy in her time – with the exception of an unfortunate case of peritonitis which had taken her by surprise – and nobody could expect her to recognize every symptom immediately – by good fortune, and by a logical alternation of doses of Epsom Salts and Castor Oil, or the fashionable equivalents. For surface wounds she prescribed Dettol and, for anything that smacked of exoticism, she would either reluctantly send for the doctor or, more frequently, discredit the symptoms and rigorously refuse to accept the validity of any illness that she could not comprehend. Some of the younger, more superstitious boys could be forgiven for believing the popular story that she could cut out a malignant tumour with the sharp edge of her tongue.

As she stood there studying Scarfe with an ostensible air of calm detachment, she was searching frantically in her brain for a medical sounding phrase that would appease Manningham who was standing over her like an invigilator. Eventually she took her heart in her hands and opined that Scarfe was suffering from nothing more nor less than nervous exhaustion and for herself advised a couple of days in bed, but benevolently (or to be absolutely realistic, desperately) suggested that to be on the safe side they might call in one of the school doctors. Which they did, while the Dame wrote to Scarfe's family (and herself scuttled to Windsor to catch the late post) to acquaint them of the indisposition ('probably a touch of hay-fever'), to advise them not to make a special journey on Friday on behalf of the invalid, but to hope that they would put in an appearance just the same on Saturday, the Fourth of June, 'by which time your son, I know, will be his usual cheerful self'. Scarfe, meanwhile, lay on his back and watched the lightning through the curtains with a strange thrill of triumph. This would teach them.

After the doctor had made his detailed examination, he had a long and intimate talk with Manningham, which was not entirely on the medical aspects of the affair. The doctor agreed that it was not the first case of the kind to which he had been privy, but it was one of the worst. The housemaster granted that excessive violence must have been used, but insisted that his first duty was to keep discipline in his house. The doctor conceded that some kind of punishment may well have been deserved but denied that any disciplinarian had the right to allow a boy's life to be endangered. The housemaster accused the doctor of theatrical over-simplification. The doctor answered that, speaking no longer in a medical capacity, he was convinced that the case was absolutely simple, cut and dried, and that the proper authorities should be informed forthwith. The housemaster denied that there was any cause to be hasty, and gave his assurance that he would in any case speak to the boys concerned very sternly. The doctor doubted whether words would be sufficient. The housemaster, losing patience, announced that he would not dare to presume to advise a doctor on the running of his surgery nor, growing imaginative, would he endeavour to instruct a surgeon where to make an incision, so he would be very much obliged if the other would similarly mind his own business. The doctor somewhat sententiously declared that humanity was his business, and he would not let the matter rest, and that Scarfe should be transferred to the sanatorium. The housemaster thanked the doctor for his professional advice and begged to terminate the interview. The doctor with pleasure acceded to this request.

As soon as the doctor had left Manningham paid a visit on Defries.

Thursday evening. No one to be beaten. Morgan and Pemberton were in reflective mood. Pemberton was smoking an Olivier, half-way out of the Library window, just in case. His dark hair was auburn with the light of the setting sun behind it and he looked unaccountably young. Perhaps it was the drawing in of the cheeks as he inhaled. Young and vulpine.

'My God, he's a poor fish, though, isn't he?' he said, 'a real fish divine, all fish excelling.'

'He's a fish,' said Morgan.

'And one doesn't feel the same sympathy for fish. When Defries was beating him, I felt just as I do when I'm seeing a lobster boiled.'

'Hungry?'

'No, you stupid bastard, objective.'

'Oh, objective; yes, of course, Objective.'

'Why, didn't *you* feel objective?'

'No,' said Morgan after a pause, 'I felt more like the lobster actually. Defries would make quite a chef.'

'Yeah. Morgan, em, do you approve of – well, of the *way* he cooks?'

'Oh yes, it's very much to my taste.' Morgan was in a strange mood. Physically he was very relaxed, but his mind was unusually alert, his imagination active. He was almost alive. He took down the cane from the picture-hook on the wall and bent it between his hands.

'A fable of our time,' he said suddenly, 'by Adrian Stuart Anstey Morgan. Once upon a time I was a great, big oak-tree growing in the forest.'

'But it's a bamboo,' complained Pemberton.

'Dageuil!' Morgan gave him a cut on the thigh. 'And the sun and the wind and the rain, shone, blew and fell on me, the mighty turmoil of the elements, and still I stood undaunted. Until one day just like any other a poor wood-cutter came into the woods, and his clothes were ragged, and there was a permanent drip on the end of his nose, and he smelt of leaf-mould, and he put his saw to the base of my trunk and began to cut into my bark. And a shudder ran through my very fibres, such pain that I would have cried out if only I had been able to. And day after day he came and the wound cut me deeper and deeper, and the pain was ... exquisite, until one afternoon just like any other he fetched hawsers and pulleys and cables and he overturned me from my roots and brought machines to cut me up and plane me down and make canes out of me—'

'Bamboos!' interjected Pemberton scornfully.

'And I was sent to the Big School, where I spent the rest of my life happily cutting up little boys quite as innocent as I had been; and one day just like any other the son of the poor wood-cutter who, by rights, should not

have been in the school at all, but for whom an exception
had been made on account of—'

The door opened and Defries was there, quite white,
and the skin stretched tautly between his nose and his
cheek-bones, his eyes brighter than ever, and Berwick was
with him. And Defries said:

'Look here, chaps, we're really in the bouillabaisse.
They had to get a doctor for Scarfe and Manningham
wants to see me at once. We're for it; we're ruddy well for
it.' There was a catch in his voice so that he sounded as if
he was either about to laugh or cry. But it wasn't a funny
situation. Berwick quickly restored a sense of values.

'The crazy bugger,' he said advancing into the room,
'almost killed that little oik. I should think he'd get the
flipping sack, wouldn't you?'

It was strange, Phillips reflected, the way he had changed
during the last few weeks. He had toughened. Looking
back on the night with Jill on the river-bank, he was
embarrassed, but not a little charmed, by what seemed to
him now his remarkable naïveté. Imagine Berwick, for
instance, letting a chance like that slip past without so
much as what Berwick would have called a 'real feel'.
It was absurd. All that fine talk wasted. She must have
thought him slow or ignorant, probably both, and it was
a wonder she had had any patience with him at all. But it
was strange that in her letters she had never complained
about his slowness or ignorance. Perhaps they weren't the
things school-girls wrote letters about and, heaven knows,
he found her letters embarrassing enough as it was. Yes,
that must be the answer because Berwick had assured him
that 'every girl wants to be laid, just can't wait to roll over
on her back' and had added, looking at Phillips more
closely, 'it doesn't really matter who the man is.'

If only the brother weren't coming for the Fourth, he

might have had a chance to make up for last time. It was probably just as well, though, that he hadn't gone too far before, because . . . and it was clear to him that certainly *that* was why she hadn't minded him being as he was. She had credited him with more sophistication than he had had. But then should he make any preparations for the Fourth, just on the off-chance that the brother could be magicked away? He'd have to ask Berwick about that too, because it would be terrible to land in a mess, and he didn't know at all what to . . . when to . . . how to . .

Then there was Scarfe. He'd been pretty self-controlled there as well, hadn't he? How he had put up with him coming crawling round like that, day after day, calling him Tom, and crapping on about religion. Well, he'd certainly got what was coming to him, and he, Phillips, for one, was glad he'd been there to see it. Yes, he was. He only wished he could have been the one to – no, he wasn't too sure that he wished that. Though, of course, he'd have to get in some practice if he were going to be Captain of the House himself. And to think that he almost *messed* with that – that—

After all he was quite one of the lads now. As soon as he had got over those initial differences, that appalling exhibition he had given during the Colours Test, that pristine greenness, he had begun to find his way around. They seemed partly to have forgiven him, not that they were exactly companionable yet, but Defries discussed his literary aspirations with him, and Berwick seemed to enjoy playing the family doctor role on embarrassing personal problems. Morgan and Pemberton he really couldn't make out, but then he never had been able to.

It had been stupid the way he had been waylaid by that crazy old maniac by the river. 'Course if it had happened a month ago, he'd have probably found himself confessing to her by now, or at least being entertained to tea and

Bible-reading. The silly old bitch. The word, forming itself of its own volition in his mind, startled him by its violence. Why did he feel so strongly? Anyway, he'd shown her that he wasn't as pi as he looked, but he'd wasted enough time talking to her as it was.

Goddamn it, he always seemed to be wasting time with people!

But as he drifted off to sleep he softened again unconsciously, his mouth lost its hard, set line and his brow grew less resolute. The taut, tense expression of the face relaxed, for it was not yet finally set in its mould. And the last thing he remembered thinking was, it *had* been a pity about the bird.

Indeed it had.

CHAPTER NINE

In the middle of the Etonian morning people disperse for Chambers. Boys run off to Rowlands for new potatoes jaundiced with margarine and Coca-Colas and soft fruit in season. Over a Strawberry Mess or a Banger they converse in their own strange tongue: 'Can you spout the Saying Lesson?', 'I'll be in P.S. if I get another rip', 'We used to get runs up to Fishy last half.' They appear unselfconscious, extrovert, happy. Masters more sedately retire to Upper School for more orthodox refreshment, including, by tradition at any rate, the Chambers Bun. There they discuss details of administration and any individual problems that may arise. It is a mysterious ceremony with something of the board-meeting, something of the military briefing, something of the bun-fight. Lower-boys will have it that they go there to booze, but lower-boys' sense of the melodramatic is stronger than their common sense. Chambers is practical, functional, teetotal.

Chambers on Friday, June the third, was a comparatively light-hearted affair, but the Headmaster looked serious enough for Passion Sunday as he bore down on Manningham. He was a short, trim headmaster with a sandy toothbrush moustache that made him appear from a distance as if his upper lip had been smeared (carefully, mind you) with meat paste. In manner he had much of the soldier and little of the scholar, but his mind was that of a society artist; that is to say, he had enough imagination to observe life objectively (and that does require imagination) as others saw it, but not enough imagination to relate it to himself. He had, if you like, flair but not vision. People admired him, but never more.

'Doctor Saunders telephoned me this morning, Manning-ham,' he said in a low, cool, sophisticated voice, 'he told a strange tale.' With his white tie and flowing gown, he seemed to Manningham like an exotic bird of prey.

'Yes, Headmaster.'

'This boy was paralysed, is that right?'

'Yes, Headmaster.'

'And severely lacerated about the buttocks?'

'Well, relatively speaking, I should say . . .'

'Severely enough to be at present receiving treatment in the Sanatorium?'

'For paralysis.'

'Manningham, let us not prevaricate.'

'No, Headmaster.'

'Have you investigated the matter? Have you dis-covered who is responsible?'

'Headmaster—' Those who knew Manningham from below, so to speak, would have been amazed at the supplication in his voice.

'Now look, Jimmy' – far be it from the Headmaster to underestimate the timing of a diminutive Christian name! – 'this is only your second half as housemaster, I believe I am correct?' Of course it was. They neither of them needed reminding of that. 'Let me give you a word of advice' – now for the epigram of which he was so fond – 'the guilty, Manningham, must suffer with the innocent.'

'You mean that Defries, my Captain, will have to go?'

'I mean that they will all have to go,' said the Head-master, dismissing a whole battalion of boys with a flourish of his gown, 'all who were present, that is.'

'Headmaster, that is my entire Library, five boys. Phillips, at least, was not in any way to blame.'

'Phillips? Oh yes, of course, the embryo Shakespeare. Literature, you know, is not frequently innocent.'

'Let me make inquiries, Headmaster. I'm not trying to whitewash them, Heaven knows.'

'Heaven may know, Manningham, but if it does it hasn't taken the trouble to inform me. If any evidence comes to light to support your charitable theories, you might let me know by tea-time. But bear in mind that to understand all is to condemn all. As for the others, if you can bring yourself to believe that guilt does exist in a Public School, their parents had better remove them tomorrow. Ah, well, back to the savageries of the Roman Empire. And Manningham' – the bird returned for a final peck – 'I'm not saying that your boys are in any way at fault. They just live out of their century, that's all. Or perhaps I do.'

Scarfe's iron bedstead lay in the exact centre of a big, white, square room in the Sanatorium. The only furniture was a bedside table on castors and a bedside chair. On the one a long, yellow, bubbling drink fizzed away, the bubbles rising and falling as silently as the hackles on a dog's back; on the other Manningham sat in a stiff-backed and embarrassed sick-room pose. Scarfe looked at the ceiling and tried to make patterns out of the cracks in the paint and the shadows cast by the plain parchment lampshade swinging in the faint draught from the barred window. He thought he could make out an enormous sow suckling her piglets, but in a sudden flurry of wind the sow rolled over and . . . he couldn't make her out any more now.

'Just for the record, Scarfe, would you mind describing to me Phillips's part in the whole affair?'

'What will happen to him?'

'Oh, nothing, nothing. We just have to thresh the matter out and then see.'

'Well, Phillips – was always very good to me,' Scarfe

went on in a hurry. 'I mean, Tom and I were going to mess together, you know, but then what with him being in the Library and everything . . .'

Scarfe's hair was perfectly parted and clung to his head like a skull-cap. It hardly improved his appearance, but the sister-in-charge was a stickler. The top button of his pyjamas was buttoned too, as if he were on parade.

'He was always very kind to me, Tom was.'

'And when they were beating you?'

'There was nothing he could have done.'

It seemed strange to Manningham that the boy was talking to him so openly. It had never happened before that any boy of his had talked informally to him like this, without a 'Sir' or anything. Manningham suddenly felt a great benevolence towards the unfortunate boy, and tried to put the kindness that he felt into his next question. In the hollowness of the sick-room the unfamiliar tone of his voice echoed back to him foolishly.

'But what exactly were you doing in his room that night, Arthur; of course, you don't need to tell me if you'd rather not.'

Scarfe's little face took on a surprised look, as if the wax had melted and set again fast, for the change was not extreme. He was surprised both at the kindness in the voice and at the housemaster's calling him Arthur (his name was Alfred). Old Mockingbird really could be quite decent after all, and, seeing the unhappy man sitting so stiffly on his cane chair in the big, white room, Scarfe had a suspicion of the truth – which no other boy had ever been sharp enough to guess at – that the housemaster was by circumstance an alone man, but not by nature. Turning his eyes back to the cracks in the ceiling, Scarfe carried this idea a stage further. Maybe we all are, he thought.

'I had gone round to talk to him,' said Scarfe, 'we –we used to talk together about religion, you see.' And then, since he knew he had no choice but to do all that he could to help Phillips, he added, exaggerating somewhat: 'We used to pray together.'

'I see,' said Manningham, wondering what he saw, 'just so long as that is all you used to do together.' He hadn't meant to put it like that. He had wanted above all to retain this queer understanding that had somehow so swiftly grown up between the two of them, but those thoughtless, insensitive words had spoken themselves and it was too late to retract them now. Scarfe had looked quickly into his face, and then looked away, and that was that. The amnesty was over. There was silence in the sick-room. They were both constrained, stiff and uncomfortable. Scarfe wished that Manningham would get up and go.

'Well,' the housemaster said at length, 'how are you feeling now, Scarfe?'

'Better, thank you, sir.'

'Well, I suppose I must be moving on.' And Manningham stood up, pushing back the chair and scraping its legs against the floor, nodded and left the room. Scarfe turned over in bed and tried to sleep. Then suddenly sat up straight and realized. He had turned over in bed! He was well again. But he didn't feel very well.

After lunch Manningham entertained the four senior members of the Library in his study. Unlike the studies of most of his colleagues (Stratton's had been typically donnish) it was immaculately ordered. The books in the ceiling-to-floor shelves were not only arranged by subject ('Greek Mythology', Major English Poets', etc.) but tapered in height from shelf to shelf. The wall-to-wall carpet was a neutral grey and the curtains were of heavy red velvet, weighted at the floor. Two glass paperweights, depicting scenes from Venice and Florence within their globes, kept all his unfiled papers severely in check. Also on the desk were packets of 'Bulldog' clips, paper-clips and drawing pins and a large-sized roll of Sellotape. Finally, there was a folded copy of Friday's *Times*, which had been briefly scanned at breakfast and refolded carefully for the evening's more detailed perusal, and a vase containing six 'Gertrude Gregory' roses. Some Sheraton chairs sat back modestly against the wall (to be brought out only for Sunday Privates) and three, huge, leather-covered, padded armchairs were grouped around the electric log-fire which glowed disappointingly in the frame of the pine-wood fireplace. Consequently anyone seeking an interview was forced to move straight to an armchair – a manœuvre which the most self-confident boy would hardly dare to attempt – sit against the wall in a position of some psychological weakness, or remain standing. They generally remained standing. Morgan, Pemberton, Berwick and Defries did. Having sent for them individually and in person, Manningham had ensured that they would have had no occasion to choose a particular line of defence. Of course he only wanted to get at the truth, but even in a Public School the truth has many facets and there are frequently – as in the best crime stories – more possible solutions to any given problem than there are problems to be solved.

The four boys looked as uncomfortable as they felt. Berwick, for example, was playing with the unfastened bottom button of his waistcoat; if anyone was at ease, Morgan was. Pemberton was not entirely at his ease. Defries was looking at his feet. Manningham sighed deeply, returned to its shelf a copy of Johnson's *Rasselas*, not without first marking the place with a bus-ticket, and then said:

'I shall not be so naïve as to suppose you ignorant of the reasons for this confrontation. I shall not do you that

injustice. However, I may as well tell you that I have just
come from Scarfe's bedside in the Sanatorium, where they
hold out a good chance of his eventual recovery. I am
sure you are all as glad to hear that as I was. That is the
pleasantest part of what I have to say; appreciate it to the
full.' He paused. 'Now what I want to know is this;
were any of you besides Defries involved in the chastise-
ment of this unfortunate boy?'

Defries, speaking out in a loud, clear voice, so that he
seemed almost proud, either of the admission or the
offence, answered:

'No. None of them, sir.'

'I see. Did the rest of you connive in it?' Then, seeing a
fleeting expression on Berwick's face, 'Did you know and
approve of his actions?'

Berwick and Pemberton added a mumbling assent,
while Morgan said:

'Yes, I think you might put it that way, sir.' Manningham turned to him sharply, but decided that it would be
unwise to take issue at this juncture. To Defries:

'Nobody else actually beat the boy but you?'

'No, sir.'

'Well, that's something at any rate.'

'Are you going to sack him, sir?' said Morgan.

'Be quiet, Morgan. Your position is hardly impregnable.'

'Is yours, sir?' said Morgan; but he said it very quietly
and only his lips were seen to move by Manningham.

'I am to see the Headmaster again at tea-time. He
thinks you should all be expelled. For my part I am
beginning to think he is right. You will none of you leave
the house this afternoon. You must cut your divisions.
You are confined to your rooms or the Library, and will
await my instructions.'

Nobody moved. Pemberton was picking his nose,

rolling the mucus between his fingers. Manningham and Morgan were glossy. After a while Berwick, shuffling his feet in the way athletes have, who find it so hard to express themselves without the help of their bodies – don't we all? – cleared his throat and said in a low voice:

'I didn't have anything to do with it.' They all looked at him, but they all ignored what he had said.

It was Morgan who broke up the party by walking briskly out of the door. At once the others felt themselves free to follow him, and did. Only Defries, at a gesture from the housemaster, remained. Manningham moved to the window and threw up the sash. A steady drizzle was falling, but the rain was so light that not a leaf trembled. They would have to postpone the cricket match, he supposed. He remembered the disturbing smell of damp, white flannels in the pavilion, teas taken early and indefinitely prolonged, the ugly blotches caused by a sudden rainstorm on the score-book. He had once almost scored a century, ninety-seven in an hour and a bit, when rain had stopped play. Now he never would. He breathed deeply a few times as if drawing in through his nostrils the nostalgia of those happy, anxious times. His breath was expelled in a long, quivering sigh. Manningham was not often sentimental.

'Sir?' said Defries in that irritatingly harsh voice of his. Manningham threw off his sentimentality and his accustomed pose of weariness left him.

'Sir? Yes, sir. What is it, sir? I'll tell you, sir,' he said, exasperated beyond endurance by the boy's interruption. A stupid, ugly, unnecessary boy, who had not been able to carry out the simplest instructions without endangering the futures of all of them. And that other one, that Scarfe, who was he to put them to all this trouble? Why couldn't he have kept his place in society, instead of pushing himself where he was not wanted? Him and his praying!

Manningham had been worried into a bad temper, and
was angry at himself for betraying so human a weakness.
'Yes, sir, you, sir, have completed your education here,
sir. We tried to teach you if not to be a gentleman, at least
to behave like one, or if even that was beyond you, at least
never to be indiscreet. You have your stupidity to thank
for bringing you to this pass; I hope you're satisfied. Were
your parents coming tomorrow anyway?'

'Yes, sir.'

'They are, sir? Good, sir. I shall telephone to them
myself, although Heaven knows I could employ my time
more pleasantly.'

'Sir, I was only carrying out your instructions in
punishing Scarfe.'

'I don't have to defend myself to you, Defries. Go and
pack.'

'I haven't got my trunk, sir.' It was typical of the boy.

'Well, get it then. From the Dame. But don't bother me
any further.'

As Defries turned to go, he knocked against the desk,
and one of the paper-weights rolled on to the floor and
splintered there. Defries bent to pick it up, but then
didn't. Instead, with a certain dignity it must be admitted,
he hurried from the room. Manningham rang a bell for the
housemaid, then took down his *Rassecas* and opened it at
at the bus-ticket. When the maid knocked and entered,
he merely said to her:

'Clear up this mess, will you, please,' and returned for a
little while to his book. He didn't even know whether it was
Venice or Florence which lay shattered on the floor.

When Phillips called on Berwick a few minutes later for
advice of a practical nature, he found Berwick lying
disconsolately curved on the window-seat of the Library,
like the prize fish on a fishmonger's slab, leafing through a

tattered copy of *Health and Efficiency* which he had confiscated from a lower-boy the previous night. His whole
attitude was one of defeat, and from the gramophone came
the scratched strains of Caruso singing the sob-stuff from
Pagliacci. Phillips knew at once that something was up, not
only with Caruso, but with Berwick himself, who was not
as a rule crazy about 'all that Classical jazz'. Phillips put
out an exploratory tentacle: 'Hallo there?' but Berwick
did not respond. Caruso did, eloquently, although Phillips
endeavoured to ignore him.

'You remember what I was telling you about Jill?'

'How could I ever forget?' This heavy, athletic sarcasm
was at least better than heavy, athletic silence. Phillips was
inspirited to pursue that matter further:

'Well, look, she's coming over tomorrow, and I wondered what I ought to do about – well, you know.' It was
seldom necessary to be explicit with Berwick on a matter
of this kind. Phillips smiled encouragingly, but it was like
smiling at a firing-squad of dispossessed mercenaries.
Phillips became concerned, as anyone might in front of a
firing-squad of dispossessed mercenaries, and inquired:

'Is there anything the matter?'

'No, no, nothing's the matter, you flipping great oaf;
we're only going to be sacked, that's all.'

'What?' – Caruso broke into a pathetic silence, and the
needle scratched unpleasantly at the end of the record.

'Sacked. Morgan, Pemberton, Defries and me, that's
all. I don't flipping know about you.'

'Sacked? What for, then?'

'Oh, hell, I don't know. Scarfe squealed or went to the
San or something. That bloody little runt! Oh, but I
forgot, he's a friend of yours, of course.'

'What happened?'

'Oh, Mockingbird called us to see him after boys'
dinner and babbled on about, oh, I don't know. Anyway,

he's seeing the Head Man this afternoon. We're hell's pushed.'

'And me?' It was a fair question you would have thought in the circumstances, but Berwick's answer was unequivocal, impractical, even rude. Phillips had never been 'one of the chaps' so far as swearing was concerned; it always sounded apologetic in his mouth; not so in Berwick's.

'And the same to your flipping Jill with her brass knobs on! If you want to do her, bring her round and I'll show you how.'

'But Berwick, shouldn't I . . .?'

'Hell, yes! Why not go and ask them for one at the School Stores?' Berwick raised himself on one elbow, tore Health from Efficiency, and flung them both into the waste-paper basket. A plump, grinning nudiste with a beach ball, but torn from shoulder to shin, gazed up in unconcern. It was obviously the end of the interview. Berwick was determined to be difficult, and who could blame him? (You couldn't really get them at the School Stores, surely not?) Never mind that, now. This other thing was the thing. If they were all going to be sacked, then . . .

Pemberton and Morgan were sitting either end of Pemberton's green upholstered ottoman, shooting poker-dice on to the space between them, when Phillips came timidly knocking at the door.

'Full house, queens on knaves,' said Pemberton, as Morgan strode across the room and flung open the door. Phillips stood there, his triangular head pale and in-quisitive and nervous, like Red-Riding-Hood beginning to see through her grandmother.

'Join the Last Supper,' invited Morgan, selecting a marron glacé, delicately, with finger and thumb.

'No thank you. I only came round to find out what all this is about.'

'Well,' replied Pemberton, 'it's about us and it's about Scarfe, but I don't believe it's about you.'

'About face, about turn, not about you.'

'Did Manningham say anything at all about me?'

'Me, me, me, me, that's all you ever think about. Why should he have mentioned you? What have you done worth mentioning? What have you done that was unmentionable for that matter?'

'My grandfather,' said Morgan, surprisingly, 'composed his own epitaph, chose his own tombstone, and was about to carve these lines on it with his own hands:

> *"Born, begat and died in bed,*
> *Talk about me when I'm dead,"*

when . . . Do you know what happened?'

'No, what?' asked Phillips, who was genuinely curious.

'Yes,' said Pemberton, and threw the dice. Two nines, a ten, a queen, and an ace. 'Shit!' Morgan frowned.

'What did Manningham talk about then?' Phillips persisted.

'This and that,' Morgan explained categorically, 'that and this. And so on and so forth.'

Pemberton got the idea. 'Il bavarda, le vieux copain. He took a stand on certain matters, and was more doubtful about others. He covered a great deal of ground, leaving no stone unturned. It was fun. A good time was had by all.'

'Isn't it always?' inquired Morgan. 'All's for the best in the best of all possible hells.'

But such an optimistic viewpoint was wasted at least on Phillips, who was half-way to his room, no wiser for all Morgan's philosophy.

Manningham was waiting in Phillips's room when Phillips returned, ready to enlighten him. He had picked up the photograph of Jill that lay, face up, on the open flap of the burry, and, when a dirty bit of broadrule had fluttered to the floor, he had retrieved it and was now reading what was written there. Phillips came in and stood waiting with his back to the fireplace. Manningham gave no indication that he was aware of him. Then, turning suddenly as in grandmother's footsteps, he handed the paper to the boy, and asked him:

'Did you write this?'

Phillips looked down in some surprise and stiffened as he recognized it:

I See Stella Sleeping

> *I did not dare to take my heart's advice,*
> *And cottage cowardice gave me control ;*
> *Control has now harshly confined my soul,*
> *And my poor soul bewails its cowardice.*
> *I did not dare to take what was my right,*
> *Though I had worked for it with all my heart,*
> *My heart and head had long since grown apart,*
> *My head would not condone my heart's delight.*
> *I would have lain with Stella as she slept,*
> *But that my head saw not the counterpane*
> *And one white hand in benediction lain*
> *Upon it. From the trembling room I crept,*
> *And Stella and the darkness I let be,*
> *Each glorying in her virginity.*

Re-read like this the poem seemed so artificial and well, yes, so pompous, that he could not understand how, last night, it had seemed so profound, so meaningful to him.

'Yes, sir,' said Phillips. Surely Manningham wouldn't imagine that . . .

'I quite like it,' said the housemaster, and Phillips could hardly credit his senses, 'but I'm really surprised at you!'

Manningham smiled, but then suddenly shied away from the poem. 'Well, anyway, I didn't come about that. I imagine you can guess the subject of my visit.'

'The subject? Oh yes, sir. How is Scarfe, sir?'

'His condition is quite hopeful.' Manningham threw this off as an unrewarding line of approach. 'But I was wondering quite simply what your part in all this business had been.'

'My part?'

'Yes. Were you, for instance, consulted as to the advisability, or otherwise, of beating Scarfe three nights in succession?'

'My opinion would not have carried any weight, sir.'

'Come, come, Phillips, did you oppose it?'

Phillips knew exactly what was at stake, and Manningham hoped that Phillips would be man enough neither to answer in pride nor from an obstinate and misplaced sense of honour. Honourable people always seem to turn out the biggest trouble-makers.

'I can't remember exactly what I said,' Phillips answered, clouding his mind, 'they all knew how I felt about it. I was Scarfe's friend.' Good boy, good boy, thought Manningham.

'He told me that, too,' he said thoughtfully, 'such close friendship on both sides and you didn't even mess together; oh, I know you were in the Library. Did you enjoy seeing him beaten? Answer me truthfully now.'

'Of course not.'

'I have never met the boy,' went on Manningham, as if to himself, 'who would not enjoy in some measure seeing someone beaten. Don't think I disbelieve you though, Phillips. I don't want to see you expelled, you know. Poets are not expendable.'

'I – I won't be expelled, will I?'

'I don't think so.' Manningham had been watching

Phillips very closely. Nothing in the conversation had surprised him. Nor the way Phillips's eyes roamed restlessly round the room, everywhere but into his eyes. 'Are your parents coming over tomorrow?'

'No, sir.'

'Pity. I should like to have spoken to them. Never mind. You *really* didn't enjoy it? Strange.' As Manningham was leaving – much to the boy's relief as it happened – he turned back and made a gesture towards the sheet of paper: 'I used to write poetry when I was about your age. I thought very highly of it, and used to leave it lying about in the hope that someone might find it and read it. Nobody did, and nobody was interested enough to ask to see it, so in the end I gave it up. One must have a public, you know.' Phillips looked up quickly, but didn't reply. Manningham went back to his work.

'Headmaster?'

'Yes, Manningham, what is it?'

'I've spoken to Phillips, and he made strong protests over the beating of Scarfe. The two of them were great friends, it seems. Scarfe himself exonerates Phillips and holds nothing against him.'

'I see. And the others?'

'All in it together. Defries, of course, was the only one actually to—'

'I see. Well look, Manningham, I want you to tread very carefully. It appears that Pemberton's father is in the habit of entertaining two of the Fellows – never mind which – and is commonly believed to – well, never mind that. Are you seeing him tomorrow?'

'Yes, Headmaster. I have made arrangements to see the parents of three of them. Mr. and Mrs. Scarfe too. The Phillipses are out of the country.'

'Well, for the sake of God and the Provost and Fellows,

go easy with the Pembertons. Look, you know where to find me tomorrow, if you want me?'

'Agar's Plough?'

'On and off, yes. And if any kind of trouble blows up, let me know at once. Blast these grammar-school boys! They tie our hands for us.'

'All right, Headmaster, I'll do that.' Manningham put down the telephone receiver and chewed a couple of aspirins. He breathed deeply and relaxed into an armchair; he gave the impression of having fallen into it from a great height.

Five minutes later he happened to notice some stray hairs on the shoulders of his jacket, and picked them off one by one. Strange. He never used to be scurfy, had always watched his diet. Even as a child he had walked unscarred among the other scabby, impetiginous children on the beach. Strange. Having first carefully removed his jacket and folded it on the arm of a chair, he walked briskly to the circular wall mirror over the mantelpiece and drove the fingers of both hands back from his temples. He shook his head violently. When he looked up a dozen or so brownish hairs were floating to the ground. Bending forward and looking out of the tops of his eyes he could just make out the beginning of a bald patch on his crown. He sat down heavily, crumpling his jacket. Well, there it was. But what a waste! What a bloody waste!

Defries was bitter as hell. And chief among his gall and wormwood was a truly British sense of injustice. Manningham had given him a free hand hadn't he? He had told him to do what he thought best with regard to that squirt, hadn't he? He *had* done what he thought best, hadn't he? Of course he had. He hurled a handful of books into his trunk, and a lump rose in his throat. He had every reason to be angry, with his whole career ruined and in pieces at his feet. The weight of the lid overbalanced the trunk and the contents poured forth to illustrate the point. He cursed Manningham and Scarfe, Scarfe especially, silently to himself; it was hard with that lump there crushing his Adam's apple to curse out loud. Of course he knew that in fact it wouldn't alter his whole career overmuch. It was his last half anyway, and the army didn't care how or when or why you left your school, providing the colour of the tie was acceptable. Oh, he might be twitted in the mess, but his father would always be there to curb any excesses. It wouldn't matter in the army. But, dammit, *here* they didn't know he was going into the army.

If he'd done anything to deserve it now . . . if he'd had any fun, then he wouldn't care, why should he care, if it had been worth it. If. Why if? Didn't he still have one more night? Wasn't he leaving tomorrow anyway? Didn't they owe him a run for his father's money? Of course they did. It was just a question of finding a suitable run.

And yet it is not easy to throw off in a minute's argument a whole childhood and adolescence of subservience and obedience. It wasn't that Defries's conscience was particularly active, he was far too angry and upset to listen to that despairing little voice, it was more that his law-abiding habits, his moral routine, his ingrown orderliness was to be outraged. So, being also irrationally fearful, he postponed the decision till nearer the bewitching hour, when he had a rational hope that he might be nearer to being bewitched into his proposed enterprise. Meanwhile, he endeavoured to put the whole troublesome business out of his mind, and became prodigiously busy completing his packing.

In the noisy, intimate darkness of the 'Lower Sixers' dormitory Jill hugged her knees and shut her eyes so

tightly that scarlet and black geometrical patterns floated
in front of her retinae. To an interested observer in the
doorway (there was none) her figure would have seemed
to be surrounded by an aura of light from the full moon
that shone benevolently, like a tolerant referee, over the
hockey field. An interested observer might have imaginatively supposed that the halo emanated from Jill
herself and, imaginatively speaking, he would not have
been far wrong. Because a visit to Eton on Saturday, the
Glorious Fourth, was no small matter for a fairly unspoilt
girl in her teens. She knew she would find sleep difficult
if she thought too much about tomorrow, but what was a
good night's sleep?, and she remained hugging her knees
for a long time. Somewhere to her right two girls were
whispering and giggling together over something that
only they – no doubt of it – could understand; close
friends to whom almost every word conjured up a memory,
an association, a shared joke. It would be many years
before they ever attained such intimacy with anyone again.
And across the room a girl was muttering in her sleep:
'For ever . . . for ever . . . in the machine age . . .' and then
'No!', repeated over and over again, fervently. The
moonlight shone on basins and jugs and photograph-
frames, and on the glass eyes of stuffed toy animals, so that
one could have been in the jungle. In the jungle in a girls'
public school? In Sussex? Why not? There are still plenty
of jungles in the world and a lot of them would be
sanctuaries next to that one. Jill hugged herself in the
jungle while the moon shone round her, and, disdaining
sleep, thought long and fondly about Tom Phillips. It
would be foolish to suppose that her thoughts were of
white chargers, or sanguinary dragons, or no end of giants
but it would be more foolish to suggest that her thoughts
were altogether unromantic . . . Nobody could stop her
romanticizing him, nobody could stop her imagining

things. It's hard to guess what she expected from Tom Phillips the next day, but, whatever it was, it was surely not too much to hope for. In the machine age. On the Glorious Fourth.

Absolutely the same moon was shining into Defries's room, but only through a slit in the curtains, as he made up his mind for better or for worse, but almost certainly for worse. And, wrapping his Paisley dressing-gown round his narrow shoulders, he stole into the corridor and tip-toed to the far end where his . . . objective lay. And if he had been going to suffer a change of heart, he was too late now, because his progress down the corridor seemed to him too fast (corridors exaggerate things) for him to have time to consider it. He wouldn't have a chance to weigh the pros and cons. By the time he'd have weighed the pros . . . he was already at Bigby's door. A card on the door said J. Bigby. A friend of J. Bigby's had added, amusingly, in pencil, 'farts here'. Defries turned the handle and went in.

Now it may seem strange, but it is undoubtedly true, that Defries had no very clear idea of what he wanted, intended or expected to do, with, to, or upon the person of the angelic Bigby. He had heard, of course, plenty of dirty stories about what people did with, to, or upon the persons of other people, but he had never quite seen himself either in the dominating or the dominated role. He had more or less left all this to the inspiration of the moment and had supposed that his powers of invention, imagination or imitation would lead him on to the most delightful and wickedest accomplishments. For he never momentarily doubted that anything as wicked as the things he supposed he would do, would be delightfully entertaining; a trap that many eminent and notorious men have blundered blithely into time and again.

Certainly the idea of force entered into his conception of things; for Defries was cruel-natured and loved to spend his time in book-shops looking at pictures of tortures and atrocities. But beyond that his ideas were vague in the extreme.

So; there stood the midnight marauder with devilry – of some sort or other – in his heart, and there lay Bigby, sound asleep and dreaming of the great day to come, and the moon – inevitably the identical moon – shone on the pair of them. Defries coughed and shuffled his feet. He was cold. Bigby turned over and buried his face in the pillow, but didn't wake up. Defries ascertained that the door was shut behind him. Then there was a kind of hiatus during which for two or three minutes nothing happened at all. Finally Defries stepped forward to the bedside and pulled back the sheet. Bigby stirred, moaned, grasped the sheet and returned it around his neck, then opened his eyes, and said in a wide-awake, everyday sort of voice:

'Yes, what is it you want?'

Defries considered: 'Well, what can you offer?' As soon as Bigby's eyes had focused, an expression not of fear so much as of contempt came into his face. To Defries's dismay, although the fag looked moderately provocative with his ridiculous self-assurance and his white throat, he also looked not a bit sacrifice-prone.

'Is this a fire-practice?' he asked.

'Not exactly,' said Defries, once again drawing back the sheet and beginning to slip out of his dressing-gown.

Bigby was now very much awake, and, shouting: 'On the contrary, you're mistaken', he leapt not only out of bed and the puzzled, lunging clutches of his fag-master, but pretty well straight out of the room itself. Out of the room, across the corridor, to where was positioned an electric bell with a glass-front, on which was printed:

'IN CASE OF FIRE, BREAK GLASS'. Which Bigby obediently did with his fist, whereupon a reverberating clangour began to re-echo from all corners of the building. Defries was there at once with a whispered, and therefore practically inaudible: 'What the Hell do you think you're doing?' to which Bigby, rather more insolently than might have been expected and quite loudly, replied: 'The explanations are all yours,' and darted back into his room, where he wedged a chair between the end of his bed and the door-handle.

Within seconds Defries found himself surrounded by curious, sleep-pitted faces – lots of substitute moons – and he was hard put to it for an explanation:

'False alarm! Go back to bed!' using his authority as the ultimate answer to all awkward questions, and they all did, grumbling and buzzing. Luckily for Defries, Morgan, Pemberton and Berwick, heavy sleepers all of them, only began to struggle towards the eye of the storm when Defries's explanation had become established fact, and so they were easily and gratefully turned in their tracks. Manningham, who arrived late, the alarm bells being muffled on the private side, took Defries by the arm:

'Was it you who set off the alarm?' he asked. Defries was quite lost for an answer. 'A very childish prank; I hope you feel proud of yourself. I should have sent you away yesterday.' And Manningham escorted Defries ungently back to his room. But Bigby, who, it must be admitted, had been listening to this encounter at the keyhole, laughed himself to sleep.

THE FOURTH OF JUNE

CHAPTER TEN

THE sun is up, big, bright, red and early, much like a Victorian suitor, but altogether too early, because the bulbous clouds come rolling in from over Maidenhead, and it soon begins to rain, hard, white and cold rain. Boys running to early school at 7.30 open their umbrellas and sail through the streets like fleets of black fishing boats racing for harbour. Humidity pours from the walls of the Drill Hall Schools and the Montague James Schools and the furled gamps rise like Excaliburs from round ponds of moisture. Swans hone through the driving rain over the higgledy-piggledy roofs of Eton.

At breakfast the forecasters get busy, but for every three optimists there is an apologetic Cassandra who speaks of troughs of low pressure and occasional bright periods in Western Scotland. His restless audience suggest sending him to a bright period. People don't want to, but they almost believe these Cassandras. The Cockneys selling blue carnations in the streets, cashing in on the tradition that this is the one day in the year when anybody may wear a boutonnière, race for shelter as their blooms begin to lose their blueness, cursing in their hearts a tradition that can fade so easily in the rain. The car-park attendants on 'Sixpenny' watch with dismay as the aristocratic green turf becomes greener still, sinister-green, marshy-green, grey-green, muddy-green and finally not green at all, and the groundsmen on Agar's Plough pile the deck-chairs higher and higher, and laugh themselves silly. In Lower Chapel cracked but Tory voices extol 'All People That on Earth do Dwell' with unusual liberalism, and in College Chapel the death-watch beetles chew away at the rafters while the Chaplain intones the prayer for the Royal Family. Wet, stiff fingers are chafed and knuckles cracked, damp bangs of long black hair drip into irreligious eyes. The Special on point duty at the Burning Bush listens to the splashing of the rain on his plastic mac and deals officiously with the early-comers. Lakes form on the Parade Ground, ponds between the Fives Courts, and Barnes Pool creeps slowly up the wall of the Public Library.

And from every corner of the Home Counties, from London, bravely from the badlands beyond, Britons who never had been and who never would be slaves, roar over inadequate roads in their great machines and splash puddle-water over yokels who, once upon a time, might have touched their forelocks, but who now make very different gestures. And they all converge on Eton in a dripping, steaming morass of mechanical perfection, swearing, sweating, grinding their gears. It is a wonderful sight. England is *en fête*.

Sir Charles, Lady and Joanna Pemberton drove up to the front of Manningham's house in a shining bright Daimler. Joanna had been driving. She was a tall, gauche creature with the most beautiful grey eyes who in any other country but England would have been much admired and most worthy of such admiration. But in her loose tweed suits or her best pink organdie evening dress, with her often pink underwear unrelated to her figure except by safety pins, she was unappreciated by almost everyone. Once she had been convincingly kissed by a ski-jumper in Switzerland and once, nastily, by an elderly uncle at a Christmas party, but these experiences had only served to make her more nervous still about life and its high-waymen. Her mother – such a mother to such a daughter! – had insisted that she learn to drive, believing that it would give her added confidence. Also it would save them the increasingly demanding necessity of finding her an escort for every party to which she was invited. At first they had been able to bribe young accountants by the promise of a particularly sustaining dinner at Crawley Hall before the dance, but, as the season advanced, and the word went round the soup-kitchens of the City and the self-contained flatlets of West Kensington and Chelsea, the dinner had had to be extended to a week-end with a shoot included, and already, by June, the terms of the offer embraced a well-paid job with one of the companies at the board of which Sir Charles Pemberton dozed, an invitation to a week's cruise on the Mediterranean yacht, or, for those with similarly placed sisters, a simple exchange system, with Sir Charles's son and heir as the reluctant ground bait. No wonder pressure had been brought to bear on the unfortunate Joanna Pemberton to take driving lessons, and no wonder, with her tortured temperament and her naked nervous system, that she drove the Daimler straight into the back of the Defries's Bentley. Well, it was lucky for Joanna that the Defries had more important things with which to concern them-selves than chromium.

As arranged on the telephone the night before, Sir Charles and Lady Pemberton went directly to Manning-ham's study for an interview 'on a matter of some urgency'. Joanna sat in the car and waited, dipping her head into the Daimler Handbook like a swan into the Thames, every time a boy came walking past. The rain dappled the windows all around her until she seemed to be in hiding behind a curtain of tears. Poor Joanna! Everyone feels for her except the strong, young, tall, young mermen in their white ties and tails. Poor Joanna! Nobody understands her at all.

Manningham welcomed the Pembertons with dignified

deference, a pose which was apt to wear a little thin by the end of the holiday, but which was still as yet splendidly maintained.

'Please take a seat,' he said, and motioned his guests to the armchairs. Sir Charles sat down at once and began to pick his breakfast egg off the front of his trousers; his wife, not so easily subdued and a genius at small talk, picked up the remaining paperweight and remarked: 'What a lovely thing!'

'Yes, isn't it?' agreed Manningham, shuddering, and wondering how best to steer the conversation into the rather murky channels that he had in mind.

'What a shame for the boys that it should be so wet!' went on Lady Pemberton, in compliance with her usual practice. First, a compliment. Then, a meteorological observation. And third, an inquiry, wherever tactful, as to the health of the other party.

'It is, isn't it?' agreed the housemaster. 'Now if I may, Sir Charles, I have something of—'

'And how are you keeping, Mr. Manningham? The worries of mid-term not weighing you down, I trust? Ha, ha.'

'Ha, ha,' agreed Manningham politely.

'Ha, ha,' added Lady Pemberton. Sir Charles looked up from his dry cleaning.

'Manningham has something to tell us,' he announced, 'let him get it off his chest.'

'Ha, ha,' continued Lady Pemberton, as politely as ever.

'Well, that is true, as a matter of fact,' said Manningham hurriedly, 'it's about Robert.' For one horrible moment he wondered if he'd got the Robert right, but there was no visible reaction, so he could breathe again. Wishing to advance the argument without being tactlessly abrupt, he explained: 'Yes, it's about Robert that I wanted to talk to you.'

'Well?'

'How is Robert?' inquired Lady Pemberton, dragging up a horde of maternal pride from somewhere.

'Well, he's healthy enough, but I'm afraid he's been involved in some rather bad trouble.' Pemberton looked up with something almost akin to interest in his dull eyes

'Robert in trouble? Oh, nonsense!'

'Well, you did ask.'

'I know I asked, but I had no idea I would hear him slandered like this.' The claws of Lady Pemberton's right hand began to curl and uncurl, a sure sign that she was in for one of her attacks.

'Slandered? Who's being slandered?'

'Your son Robert.'

'Oh, so you admit he *is* my son.'

'Whose else could he be? The Prime Minister's?' But Sir Charles had lost interest again – it had only been token resistance – and gave a gesture of resignation, which was easier for him than for the Prime Minister, to Manningham. With great patience and much lucidity the latter went on to describe the circumstances of the case to the mother. She greeted each new revelation with furious disbelief or with icy scorn, until she was blowing alternatively hot and cold like an exotic geyser. Eventually she flung a gout of steaming fury a mile high into the air.

'How can you expect me to believe such atrocious, scandalous lies? Who cares about a grammar-school boy anyway? The newspapers shall hear of it, and don't imagine I haven't influence with the Fellows. You can't expel a boy out of petty spite . . . There's not a word of truth in it . . . Your name and the name of the school—'

'College,' corrected her husband.

'—will stink when I've finished with you – Take me to the Headmaster. I demand to see the Headmaster.'

It was this last command, accompanied by a fearsome

lowering of the head and rolling of the eyes, almost pawing of the ground, that most affected the unfortunate Manningham, who held up a restraining hand:

'I can't do that, my dear madam. He will be entertaining . . . He will be at Speeches . . .'

Lady Pemberton seized the remaining paper-weight and flung it to the floor. 'Take me to the Headmaster! Speeches don't begin for half an hour. Take me to the Headmaster!'

'You had better do what she wants,' advised her husband in an undertone, 'she'll get worse.'

So Manningham did.

If the Glorious Fourth of June was heaven for the débutantes, it was certainly purgatory for Mr. and Mrs. Geoffrey Scarfe. In the ordinary course of events, that is. A sort of worse than purgatory in which they squirmed on the sharp spike of fashion watched (so it seemed) with gleeful spite by the red, ogling eyes of a milliard devil-reporters and crumbling columnists. They experienced the same feelings as the brave Welsh miner who, having by intuition saved his comrade from a death worse than fate, travels to Buckingham Palace to receive the George Medal. No intuition helps him there, and no comrade comes to *his* rescue, but toppered and togged and stiff and starched he faces not only his monarch, who is perhaps not unsympathetic, but also his country, as represented by British Pathé and Movietone. His courage sinks into his spats. The wife and family with him and the little girl who had looked forward to it so much wonders why daddy had to go down the mine. It's easy to be stupid after the event. Such feelings Mr. and Mrs. Scarfe would share – marriage being a sharing – annually, on the Fourth of June. He would don his pin-stripe and she her three-piece, and their Vauxhall would be rubbed and polished and oiled almost as thoroughly as Mr. Scarfe himself. That was their annual more than purgatory, and if it was more than purgatory for them, what may I call it for their son?, but this year things were different because this year they didn't come to celebrate. They came to fetch their son home, if the Sanatorium considered it wise, for the Dame had followed up her 'hay-fever' letter with a telephone conversation to the effect that after this rather nasty virus infection, a recuperative holiday in the Norfolk air would do him the world of good. And so this year they didn't intend to waste their time celebrating the birthday of any German king.

They puttered up to the door of the red, antiseptic Sanatorium and, even as they rang the bell, their Norfolk whiff, their Norfolk tang, was dissipated in that wholesome, desiccated air. Scarfe was up and dressed, smarter than usual with true medical orderliness, and quite able to move his limbs almost fluently again, waiting for them in a room provided for that purpose, reading magazines provided for that purpose and supervised by the sister, a white, uncomfortable sort of person who had a habit of coming upon you unwelcome and unexpectedly like an early frost. She received Mr. and Mrs. Scarfe with a great deal of polite enmity, and handed over their son as if (in some ways) she was the usurped ambassador of a decadent, imperialist power handing over to the new, independent president the keys of the embassy. You don't deserve them, you won't know what to do with them, but my instructions were to hand them over to you, and, by Jove, it's my solemn duty to obey instructions, however distasteful they may be to me personally.

'Keep him warm and let him rest,' she said, nipping introductions having been effected by the receptionist, 'and above all avoid asking him too many questions. You will find that he is still in a highly emotional state.'

'But hay-fever? The virus infection?'

'There were certain nervous complications. Your boy is highly strung, and what with his lowered resistance, and so on . . . but we'll send you full details of that in due course.' And then in a confidentially lowered voice: 'It is better not to discuss these things in front of the boy. We must beware of encouraging any morbid hypochondria.'

Mr. Scarfe brushed a few flakes of scurf off a broad, navy-blue shoulder and assured her that he quite understood and would follow her instructions to the letter; which assurance gave an even more cynical curve to the lips of the sister. However, her part in the ceremony had been performed without a hitch and that was that.

'We will take him straight home,' said Mrs. Scarfe, laying a pastry-rolling hand on her boy's head.

'That would be extremely wise,' returned the sister, and instructed the receptionist to show them out. As they left Mr. Scarfe had a feeling that the rhythm of the interview had been unsatisfactorily concluded, remarked:

'We really are most grateful to you for looking after our son . . .' but the lady in white had turned on her sensible heels and vanished with a look that seemed to read: 'Well, so long as your gratitude has been adequately sterilized, I am perfectly happy to put it into safe keeping for you.'

The Scarfes, having relieved their minds by deciding, in the interests of their son, to cancel their interview with Manningham booked for later in the day, left Eton in the cosy leatheriness of their Vauxhall, meeting many glossier cars as they drove away, and they splashed them, and they were splashed by them, and the rain eased off a little, and the boy huddled into his rug, cold, not wanting to be seen, not wanting to be spoken to, not wanting anything very much.

Chapel was over. The Headmaster was calling Absence –
that is, paradoxically, a roll-call of those present – from
the steps of College Chapel. Behind him stood his own
little retinue, with grey-check trousers instead of machine-
guns but with the regulation eyes of steel, the Captain of
the School and the Captain of the Oppidans, magnificent,
ethereal creatures, the sort you see on Postage Stamps,
contemptuous and unapproachable as Buddhas. On the
worn cobbles of School Yard itself boys awaited the calling
of their names, and doting families their boys. Doe-eyed,
sloe-eyed boys, crimped boys and crumpled ones, boys of
no mean intelligence and boys of congenital idiocy, a
cross-section of rich and noble boys, in fact, massed and
swarmed under the Founder's Statue, gone green and
white with age and bird-droppings. Lady Pemberton, her
arms flailing like windmill sails, pummelled her way to
the forefront of the press, and, bobbing in her wake, came
her husband, fatalistic and for the moment ironically
inclined, and an extremely harassed Manningham.
Names and acknowledgements in a monotonous and
endless series of responses floated over the heads of the
crowd. 'Earl of Appleby . . . heresir, Appleton . . . heresir,
Arbuthnot . . . Arbuthnot . . . heresir.' Morgan and
Pemberton, standing together and laughing over somebody's indiscretion, 'just what you'd expect in Tuggery,'
were petrified into immobility as they saw the little
procession chuffing through the crowd.

'Here we wait,' panted Lady Pemberton, grinding to
a halt almost in the shadow of the Headmaster's whiskers,
and still the names floated over their heads: 'Cadell . . .
heresir, P. Campbell . . . heresir, S. Campbell . . . heresir,
Carey . . . heresir.' A gust of wind caught the Headmaster's
mortar-board and flirted with it skittishly. 'Proctor . . .
heresir, Prodger-Stevens . . . heresir, Proops . . . oh,
heresir.' The last drops of rain fell and the clouds glided

like a smoked-glass screen across the sun. The infernal warbling of a motor-bike in the High Street rose to an intolerable pitch, and then the driver changed gear, and the machine whined away towards Slough, its spiritual home. 'Yarborough . . . heresir, Yeats . . . heresir, Zimmerman . . . heresir.' Zimmerman, as always, was the signal for a burst of conversation from the score or so boys who had remained until the end, and the visitors wondered if that really could be all. Zimmerman himself, a self-conscious boy, scuttled off, scarlet with embarrassment. Lady Pemberton, recognizing that her moment had come, darted forward to accost the Headmaster, but at the very last moment, when she might have grasped him by the lapels and shaken him (looked, too, as if she might, and the two men behind her, united in their anxiety by the bond of sex, feared that she really would), the Headmaster turned away, smiled graciously, and bowed low to . . . Royalty! Real, honest-to-goodness Royalty! And Lady Alison retired a few steps in confusion, for she, the more or less invincible she, had been silently subdued by the dirtiest trick providence could possibly have played. Somewhat daunted, the small procession tagged on behind Royalty and Authority with Manningham now at its head. Once the Headmaster, feeling no doubt the six sharp eyes boring into the fleshy part of his neck, turned and fixed Manningham with a disapproving ogle and added to this no more than a flutter of the fringes of the hands as a gesture of abrupt dismissal; and then the housemaster turned to his guests and told them:

'Take out your boy and Morgan too. I'll talk to Him later.'

'Is that a promise?' snapped the lady.

'My dear Lady Pemberton, I shall do what I can.'

'You better had; for, if you don't, I certainly shall. I am not tamed yet, sir.' And she and her tamer turned away to where Morgan and Pemberton were frisking by the School Notice Board. Manningham wrapped his gown round him like a black shroud and almost sprinted past the School Office towards his house. Where other interviews awaited him . . .

Phillips crouched in the Odd Job Man's room where he had a commanding view (although it was no luxury hotel in there), a sweeping vista of the road leading to and from Manningham's. Around him were shelves of cricket-boots, and on a work-bench behind him an improvised last, studs and nails, shoe-whitener, gave Holmesian or even Watsonian clues to one of the Odd Job Man's less odd occupations. But it was always winter, or autumn anyway, in the Odd Job Room to this extent that caked or mouldering mud from the last few football seasons clung to every board, to every crack, to every cranny. And the smell of mud confounded his nostrils and the mud particles crept under his fingernails. However, from there he really did have an awfully good view of the road. He had raced back from Absence to take up his position, but there was still no sign of Jill or her brother or her brother's car or anything that might remind him of her or her brother or her brother's car or the night of the midnight swim. Joanna Pemberton still sat there doggedly, though the curtain of tears had now parted and the Daimler Handbook had yielded up its secrets, but the dented Defries car had driven away, taking Defries with it, Phillips guessed. Twenty-three cars, excluding two trades-men's vans which he didn't count, passed in front of Manningham's but none of them contained Jill. He would start counting again from scratch. This kind of excite-ment was quite new to him. In much the same way he had counted the cars outside the Hertfordshire Doric entrance to his Prep School a few years ago, but that excitement had been pure excitement. This was savoury; this was spiced. If he thought of her too long and too vividly, it was as if he were being dismembered and deviscerated, until he was nothing but a quivering piece of masculine flesh. It was a pleasant but infinitely dangerous feeling, and, if it persisted, he would have to try to cast her out of his mind and think of something else. Like the first Test Match. He dared not allow his imagination free play. The twentieth car of the second series stopped at the front entrance to Manningham's, or as near as it could get, and Phillips stiffened. However, he was sufficiently self-aware to observe that he stiffened. The car was a low-slung, sky-blue Alfa Romeo coupé, but the fawn hood was up and the side-screens fastened. To Phillips's intense disappointment it was not Jill, it was not Jill's brother, who climbed languidly out, but the only person who could climb languidly out of an Alfa Romeo coupé, the Honourable Mrs. Alethea Berwick in person, accompanied by, or more or less understudied by, her dressmaker's sister. Phillips, of course, only knew who it wasn't, and sighed heavily, and took it very much to heart. It. Poor old Phillips.

Alethea and her understudy teetered into Manningham's and along to Berwick's room, where Berwick sat idly fiddling with his flies. Gliding across the room as if on wires. Alethea embraced her son in an almost convincing display of affection. She really was fond of him, but the expression of such a domestic feeling was something in which she was not practised. Berwick naturally became acutely embarrassed and at length disentangled himself from her with a whispered:

'Mummy, please.' Alethea patted her spherical coiffure into shape and cried out in delight:

'Such an affectionate greeting! What had I done to deserve so loving a son?' but then added warningly:

'No, don't tell me.' The understudy, nervous that she might forget her lines, although quite confident of her part, smiled beguilingly, letting a few small teeth glide over the lower lip in the approved fashion, and huskily, throatily, hallo-ed. Berwick hastily erected stakes bristling around his outer defences and asked his mother unceremoniously:

'Who is this, then?' and the mother, proud of the rabbit which had popped so obediently from the hat, replied:

'Why, this is Beatrice. You remember, I wrote to you about Beatrice.'

'Oh yes, Beatrice.'

'Say hallo to Beatrice, George.'

'Hallo, Beatrice.'

'Hallo,' said Beatrice with triumph. Why, she was word-perfect!

'And who is Beatrice?' Alethea sighed. If the dear boy was going to be difficult . . .

'What a pretty room!' said Beatrice, beginning to improvise.

Alethea looked daggers at her lieutenant, who quailed.

'Now, Sugar.' Alethea sat down on the bed and addressed the pillow; it would save her son the necessity of having to look her in the eyes while making his answer. It was tantamount to begging him to lie if the truth was to be unpalatable. 'What is all this horrid business about?' Berwick had neither the energy nor the imagination to deny the truth, however, let her play with the pillow all she liked.

'Mockingbird is going to sack me because I was present when that dirty little oik was beaten up,' he said succinctly.

'Darling, it all sounds most terribly decadent and thoroughly outré and I must admit that much of what you say is quite beyond little me, but I think I catch the *essence* of your meaning and I really can't allow that grotesque little man to behave so absurdly. Will you show me his *spoor*, my own, so that I can *ferret* him out.' Alethea wrinkled her nose in a passable metropolitan imitation of a ferret, lowered her head anthropophagously, and sniffed into the passage like a Bisto Kid. Beseeching, placating, pleading, Berwick followed at her stiletto heels and, to save himself the nightmare of a chance meeting with (worst of all) a lower boy, chivvied her through the green, baize door that abutted on to the private side of the house, and towards the entrance to Manningham's study.

'Mummy will nip him in the bud,' trilled Alethea, 'while you return to that enchanting little monster. She will be *pining* away.' Then, flinging open the door imperiously, Alethea marched into Manningham's study, her voice vibrating with thrilling persuasion as she murmured:

'Now, Mr. Manningham, don't be a bear, I really must chew things over with you.'

Manningham and his two guests looked up from the lower depths of their armchairs in astonishment. For a moment Alethea lost countenance, and the sparkling fingers of her outstretched hand fell to her side and dangled there, clutching feebly at the air. Then, as a reviving breath of her new perfume, 'Pour L'Amour d'un Nain,' tormented her nostrils, she recovered, and continued, but somewhat less vibrantly:

'Don't *rack* me with suspense. Introduce me to these irresistible friends of yours, you old buffalo.'

'Lord and Lady Bigby,' said Manningham, rising unsteadily, 'may I introduce the Honourable Mrs. Alethea Berwick.' And then, for quite a long time, nothing happened.

Well no, that's not exactly true. That can never be

true. The pendulum of the grandmother clock, for
instance, kept swinging, each time shortening its parabola.
The dust danced and the roses wilted invisibly in their
vases. Or to give a further example the living organisms
that live and eat in the organs of each one of us, in the
stomach, in the intestines, even in the organs of Britishers,
they kept on their endless battle for survival (or search
for truth) inside Manningham, Alethea, and the Bigbys.
But in spite of the clock and the dust and the roses and
the parasites, nobody said anything for perhaps ten
seconds. And then the Bigbys, who were meticulous in
their observance of the niceties of social intercourse, who
knew how to behave in short, rose and said well, how nice
it had been to have had this little chat, and how glad
they had been to hear such a good report of dear Jeremy,
and thank you and good-bye. And even – for they really
were meticulous – how nice to have met you, Mrs.
Berwick.

Standing proudly with her long fully-fashioned legs
astride on her own battlefield after the rout of the Bigbys,
Alethea let her rough cat's tongue moisten those lips of
hers that were pink and sensual as slugs in the sun.

'Such *un-us* people,' she sighed, 'ah, the indescribable
vulgarity of a peerage!' And then moving to the arm of
the chair from which Manningham had risen: 'Now,
you old bison, tell Alethea all about it. Why are you so
cross with my beautiful son? He's all I've got, you know.'
Manningham put his hand to his forehead. For him the
festival was proving even worse than he had anticipated.
He felt giddy.

'Excuse me,' he said, and sat down.

'Oh, you poor creature,' Alethea put a sympathetic
hand to his, 'you are very pale. It's absolutely wrong
that these *unnecessary* people should be allowed to tire
you so.'

'I'm all right,' growled Manningham, unlocking his hand and moving to the drinks' cupboard.

'Oh thank you, darling, I'd love an utterly dry sherry.'

'Well, you can't have one.' Manningham gasped. Who had said that? Had he said that? To a parent? He must be taking leave of his senses. Stratton's parting words to him re-echoed in his mind's ear: 'Parents are like God, Manningham, ubiquitous and omniscient. It is blasphemy, to be rude to either.'

Manningham apologized: 'I beg your pardon. You're right. I am tired today,' and handed her a small Oloroso in a big glass, 'now what else may I do for you? I am afraid my decision about your son is irrevocable. The Headmaster agrees that we have no choice in the matter.' But Alethea just smiled brightly.

'You're not used to drinking, are you?' she purred. The housemaster drained his whisky. 'You just couldn't have retained that wonderful boyish figure of yours, if you'd taken to alcohol.'

Olé! Now there she had touched his feelings. To think that, in spite of the cut of his suit, she had noticed . . . So what if he was vain about it! But he must make one thing quite clear:

'Well, just so long as you realize that I cannot in any way alter my decision.'

'Oh, it is the serious one, isn't it?' It was indeed, but try as he might when she looked at him like that, he couldn't stop the corners of his lips quivering. 'Well, I'm sure whatever George did, and believe me I *know* what boys are like, they have absolutely no consciences, wasn't meant viciously. He's really, basically, one of the sweetest-natured—'

'I hardly like to disillusion you—'

'Well, what did he dooo?' She oooed like an owl, and opened her eyes almost as wide.

'He didn't do anything exactly, but—'

'Nothing! What a severe brute it is then to turn away a boy for doing nothing!' With tiny, sparrow steps Alethea had been hopping towards Manningham who now found himself trapped between the drinks' cupboard and the bookcases. As she made this last accusation she slipped her white hand into the waistband of his trousers (against his stomach towards his heart, so to speak) and added plaintively: 'And I'm sure it isn't really a severe brute.'

Had he protested at once, Manningham might have saved himself and the situation. He would then have been the decent citizen crying out against assault and outrage; but, for the life of him – and he had been living it up a bit already that morning – the only thing he could think of to say, so aghast was he, was: 'Madam!' and that would have sounded comical and most horribly Victorian. He paused. And then it was too late. Anything he said now would seem, after such a brief but profound intimacy, like little more than the fluttering protest of convention, or in another word, like condonement. Finally, in desperation he howled:

'Really, Mrs. Berwick!' and darted to the other corner of the room, but it was not enough, because she was grinning, grinning, grinning at him now, and Heaven knew what would come of it all. Alethea moved in for the kill, and her eyes were gleaming like ferret's eyes . . .

With a noise like a *basso profundo* vomiting his breakfast in an echo-chamber (a most fulfilling noise for the connoisseur), the supercharged Triumph drew up next to the Alfa Romeo. The sun had at last appeared and was glistening as well on the Pembertons' Daimler, which fortress Joanna had finally been persuaded to vacate by the promise of a visit to the art exhibition at the Drawing Schools; Joanna, like so many English girls with her limitations, had leanings towards Art. Out of the Triumph and into the sun stepped the veritable Sun God himself, and the sun glowed with especial favour, showing him its paces, on his brilliantine. In Phillips's mud-infested eyes the privilege seemed to be extended to the Sun God's sister who climbed daintily on to the tarmacadam with just a whisper of petticoat and smiled gratefully at the Sun God who was holding the door open for her. Phillips was horribly conscious of the contrast between these ethereal creatures and his clayey self, but beating his arms at his side like a rooster, he emerged from the Odd Job Underworld and went to meet his Persephone.

'Hallo, old boy,' said the Sun God, holding out a spanner of a hand, 'sorry to be late and all that, eh?'

'Hallo. Hallo, Jill.' Phillips looked boldly into Persephone's eyes, and noticed how the white was all smudged with blue. Of course, the other time it had been dark. Jill's eyes were the first to fall, and she too held out a hand and greeted him shyly. Then she introduced him to brother Roderick – that was the Sun God's name – and Phillips asked Roderick if he had been doing any more swimming, and Roderick said no, no, there wasn't time. He was in the Royal Artillery. The Royal Artillery, eh? Yes, the Royal Artillery. Very nice, the Royal Artillery. Very noisy, Jill suggested, and everybody laughed. No, they didn't spend quite all their time shooting off guns, ha ha, and again everybody laughed.

'Well, look here, old man, I've got to go and see a chap in Hinton's, don't you know, so I'm sure you two'll excuse me. Do without me for a while, eh, ha ha?'

Ha ha. The Sun God strode off, umbrella at the slope, and natives everywhere scuttled into the shadows deciding that there was no hurry for independence, no really, they didn't mind waiting, quite all right. The sun went in.

And the other two were surely glad to see him go – that

was what they had been waiting, hoping against hope, for
– but now found that they had to entertain themselves;
and they didn't know how to begin. Jill took Phillips's
hand and pressed it.

'Oh, Tom, I've been thinking about you an awful lot,'
she said, 'thank you for writing such sweet letters.'
Phillips wished Berwick had been there to see and hear
that. He also wished Berwick was there, invisible, at his
elbow, to advise him how to proceed after such an
auspicious beginning. 'Nothing to it,' Berwick would have
assured him, 'so long as you choose your moment right.'
Yes, but how would he know when to . . . how to . . .
what to . . . Oh dear, how wonderful it would be to be
experienced.

'Would you like to see my room?'

'Would I be allowed to?'

'Well, families are. And we're almost like brother and
sister, aren't we?' The spirit of Berwick, summoned to
his elbow, chortled crudely. Jill just smiled prettily.

'Then I would like to see it, brother Tom.'

As they climbed the stairs, brother Tom pointed to the
muddy Underworld.

'I waited for you in there. It seemed like years.'

'Perhaps it was only six months.'

Phillips was very glad that Jill was climbing the stairs
in front of him; he liked her ankles particularly and at
once he was able to recapture some of the excitement he
had felt while waiting down there. The arrival itself, like
all arrivals, in spite of the presence of a deity, had proved
itself a bit of an anti-climax.

'They were all terribly jealous of me at school, you
know,' Jill went on. 'I half thought they'd scratch my
eyes out in breakfast this morning.'

'I'm jolly glad they didn't,' said Phillips.

Partington had thoroughly set his room in order after

breakfast, but Phillips had instructed him casually to leave on the table two or three text books and his Shakespeare. He himself had positioned, half-hidden among some note-books, the poem about Stella so that Jill might find it if she might. The bed, as always during the day-time, was folded up against the wall, concealed by a blue curtain with forget-me-nots on it. Jill stopped on the threshold in surprise – a habit most women have, either subconsciously from a wish to be carried over it or because it's just a habit women have – and asked:

'Is this all yours?' Phillips nodded. 'You mean to say you have it all to yourself?'

'Absolutely.'

'Phew! But . . . but where do you sleep?'

In reply Phillips, more or less digging the transparent Berwick in his unsubstantial ribs, unfolded the iron bedstead and let it down slowly into place. 'Try it,' he said. Jill laughed:

'Silly!' but none the less she did sit down a little sceptically on it, and then, gaining in confidence, began to bounce charmingly. Phillips was sitting next to her on the bed, upright, serious, a complete contrast had anyone been watching them (the translucent Berwick, perhaps?). Because she was all laughter and smiles, quite innocently unselfconscious, while the other, so very much changed in the last month, was watching her with a desperate intensity as though that simple action of hers would explain away all the secrets of the universe. And some tiresome people, I suppose, would claim that it could. Suddenly blacking out his mind to everything but the moment itself, Phillips threw himself sideways on to her and buried his face in what turned out to be her neck. He could feel, and tried to feel, and did feel the whole length of her body under his, especially as she at once, amazed and confused, began to struggle against him. She kept on calling out: 'No, Tom, don't! No, Tom, don't!' until he had realized his terrible blunder and started to wonder how to save himself the worst of the embarrassment to come. The invisible Berwick was not even there any more, and Phillips stumbled to the window, murmuring: 'I thought you wanted me to.'

Jill was almost in tears, but all she could find to say was: 'Look how you've crumpled my dress,' which was true enough, but not of much importance in the chicken-licken world about her ears.

The real and visible Berwick sat glumly on a chair and stared across at the dressmaker's sister who sat glumly on a chair and stared across at him. They had given up any attempt at passing the time, which would pass anyway, and had been like that for a long time now. Once Beatrice had made a courageous attempt with the whispered inquiry, eyes downcast, hands demurely folded:

'Would you like to see some photographs?' and when Berwick's eyes had lit up (why? what did he *expect*?) she had produced numberless pictures of dirty, pot-bellied children, obscurely related to her, crawling about on a pebbly beach in what appeared to be a thick fog. Berwick had not even had enough spirit to do more than return them with a mumbled 'Lovely', before relapsing into torpor. And so they sat, while the great ones of the world did whatever they were told, and the stars in their courses, obedient to something, spun through space, unregarded, ungratified, to no apparent purpose.

Alethea ran her hot, wet, serviceable mouth round and around Manningham's right ear, stopping every third circuit or so to chew at the ear-lobe, like a racing-car coming into the pits for refuelling. It was remarkable that they had so quickly come to terms, but not so remarkable if one had been exposed to the full fury of Alethea's will. She would not be thwarted, and was not, and never would be while she had her faculties. Of course, it had been a lucky chance that had promoted to her Manningham's figure, but no one could have accused her of not playing her luck; so far.

'My dearest, is there nowhere we could be alone?' she waved a hand vaguely at the leaving photographs of old boys, framed and mounted, that gaped down on them from the walls. 'Doesn't it send shivers down that *adorable* spinal column – I feel sure that it is quite adorable – to have them all watching you . . . at this moment?'

'Please, Mrs. Berwick, I beg of you, don't *do* that. I have an interview with Sir Reginald and Lady Hawk in . . . Good God, they're overdue already. Alethea. Please don't do that.'

'Really not?'

'No, no, please.'

'Why not?'

'Oh, because, because.' Manningham sounded as if, with one more twist of the rack, he would betray the entire Resistance movement. Alethea took a breather.

'Then you will promise me to see the Big White Chief – he is white, isn't he, my angel? – about that darling boy of mine? And you will promise not to turn him into the cold, cold snow; I couldn't bear the boredom of sending him to one of those unprincipled Swiss schools, although of course he does love his skating.'

'No, I can't promise. It's ridiculous to make a promise that—'

'But Alethea made a promise, didn't she? And she is never too terribly prodigal with her promises. During the fireworks . . . And she feels *instinctively* that she will keep her promise.'

Manningham glanced wildly at the grandmother clock.

Stratton would have had no advice for such a situation; poor old Stratton! Maybe it was the whisky, but he suddenly felt like cocking a snook at Stratton and all he stood for. 'Ubiquitous and omniscient.' Pompous old fool! Look where it had landed him. A cottage that flooded every winter and a pension of a few hundred a year. Promise, promise, promise. Pemberton and Morgan, and now Berwick, and the Headmaster entertaining Royalty! And the Hawks . . . Anything would be preferable to them finding him here, like this. A cabinet minister. An art-collector. A man of parts.

'Yes, yes, yes,' he cried distractedly, gasping for breath, which was hard to come by just at the present, 'I'll do anything you want, only go away now, please?'

'Till tonight then,' said Alethea, in a stage whisper rearranging her décolletage, and slunk towards the door, just as a governmental rap upon it almost cracked the paint.

'I can read palms,' said Beatrice desperately, 'would you like me to tell your fortune?'

'Why have you changed so much, Tom, what have they done to you?' asked Jill.

And Manningham swept his hair from his brow and tightened his braces and offered Sir Reginald Hawk a drink.

CHAPTER ELEVEN

JUNE THE FOURTH is under way. Chugging into the afternoon with its complement of colourful pleasure-lovers and camp-followers like a Mississippi steam-boat. And an elegance, an ease, a pastoral urbanity; Sir Daphnis and Lady Chloë having déjeuner sur l'herbe. Cartwheel hats and brown Italianate backs and eyelashes like porcupine-quills. Squadrons of stiff upper lips covering regular Fort Knox teeth; round, sloping, Chippendale shoulders and elderly young men carrying their paunches proudly like women pregnant for the first time. Truly we are a favoured nation, praise the Lord . . . And everywhere the Fats Waller black and blue; one could imagine *him* on a Mississippi steam-boat, but here . . . Tanned stockings over tanned legs; Durante playing Shylock in a false nose. And one may observe a strange kind of unilateral Oedipal complex common in the public schools; mothers proud of their sons, sons ashamed of their proud mothers, and fathers . . . bring down my grey hairs in Surrey to my grave.

And there are 'Speeches' in Upper School. Sixth-form boys in court dress with buckled knee-breeches declaim passages from the world's literature and history with the greatest self-assurance. Only they are inclined to be morbid this year. Major-General Gordon is resurrected once again from his disturbed rest at Khartoum. Well, that's the price of heroism. 'And some there be which have no memorial . . . their bodies are buried *in peace*' [my italics]. Pushkin's dying Tsar takes leave of his son and the National Cemetery at Gettysburg is dedicated anew. In such small ways Great Britain still does her bit to retain the balance of power. There is Siegfried Sassoon's 'The Death-bed', 'Porphyria's Lover' by Browning and the 'Lines on the Death of Doctor Swift'. Dr. Faustus is carried down to hell, there is an excerpt from Dante's *Inferno* and finally Bossuet's 'Méditations sur le brieveté de la vie' sort of sums it all up. And the ζηρυξ prompts and the dust rises and the Lower Master sneezes into his gown.

And there is cricket on Agar's Plough. At times a still life in sun and shadow that no academy in the world would reject, at others poetry in motion; George Herbert, perhaps:

'Church bells beyond the stars heard, the soul's blood,
The land of spices, something understood.'

Not much, of course, is understood by the majority of the crowd, but here and there is a rapt figure, aloof, initiated. The majority are inconsolably bored by the cricket – yet it's an exciting enough match – without that ability to relish boredom, which would be such a rare and wonderful gift at a christening. Only a very good and intelligent fairy would think of it.

But above all the scene is English. Though just across the Slough road lies the big field called Mesopotamia and the little stream called Jordan, these names mean nothing, today of all days. And if, in the morning papers there are uncomfortable reminders of barbed wire and displaced persons, of lynchings in the American South or of tanks Unten Den Linden, well the newspapers are cocked into hats to keep the sun off or mats to keep the damp out; they serve their purpose. The broad-swelling buttocks of a quantity surveyor make pulp of the crisis headlines; which is just as it should be. The battle of Waterloo was won here, remember? Don't we *deserve* a rest?

The wind rises and tries itself out in tentative gusts across Dutchman's. Mustn't make its début until quite ready. Deck-chairs and mothers begin to flap; marquees and marquesses take the strain. Queues form outside the lunch-tent, where melon, salmon, chicken and strawberries await their more or less ultimate destiny. A chicken has not lived in vain if it has lodged for a few hours in the entrails of a gentleman. There are those – there always are – who picnic in the car-parks and wash down their Fortnum's hampers with Moët et Chandon Champagne, but the hermits and recluses leave Eton altogether for the ascetic linen of the Hind's Head at Bray or the unpretentious crystal of the Compleat Angler at Marlow. Well, well, good appetites to them all, and healthy livers!

At lunch-time on the Fourth of June Manningham was quite the worst-fed man in the parish of Eton, and, if anyone deserved his meal, it was Manningham – although truly to date he had not actually accomplished much. But we live in a Little Tommy Tucker world of mean rewards for brave endeavour. Specifically his entire collation consisted of a Fox's Glacier Mint, good-naturedly tendered to him by Lady Hawk, who had a generous sympathy with a man who looked so much as her father had once looked, tired beyond his years, and a confiscated packet of rather stale Maltesers, which had reappeared mysteriously in the top drawer of his desk. With these rattling in his bowels, and the Hawks swiftly and contentedly dispatched to join their reputedly regenerate son, Manningham had set out once more on his search for a solitary Headmaster. There was a lot at stake.

Firstly, his reputation and career. If he was unable to persuade the Headmaster to keep Pemberton (and presumably Morgan) at the school, and Lady Alison Pemberton was as consistent as she was violent, then the resulting scandal would certainly mean the end of

J. F. Manninghams'. And it would be difficult now to
find that position with I.C.I. or Unilever's; the Appointment Boards and Selection Committees were so unfairly
prejudiced against young men of thirty-seven without
qualifications or experience. And second, there was his
metabolism. After the interview with Alethea his body
was throbbing like a dog stroked the wrong way, and, if he
was unable to give her the assurance she demanded, which
assurance he had so rashly and so involuntarily promised
her, he was convinced that *her* promise too would be
forfeit. And really, after waiting so long and coming so
close, he was not at all sure that his body could take a
disappointment of that kind. His blood was already
pulsating and coursing through his veins like sap, and he
felt that if he were to be denied now, he might – well, he
might burst, and bespatter Buckinghamshire with his
heart and liver and lungs and lights. It was June, wasn't
it? and he was a man, wasn't he? and he gnashed at the
Maltesers.

Brushing aside his desk diary which bristled with the
names of predatory parents so far unappeased, and
Sellotaping an envelope to the door ('Indisposed, sorry,
no interviews' – how Stratton would have shuddered at
that!) Manningham made for the Headmaster's house.
But he was too late. As he stumbled to the threshold of
the cloisters' entrance he was just in time to see the backs
of Royalty shaking themselves out of their raincoats, a
sight for sore housewives, and the stern face of the Headmaster, eyebrows drawn down into an urgent pantomime
of dismissal, turning to him blackly. Manningham tried to
torture his wonderfully inexpressive features into an
expression of supplication verging on distraction. To the
Headmaster he appeared merely jaundiced. A housemaid
in a frilly apron slammed the door in his face.

The lunch-hour was a pleasantly leisurely one for most

of the merrymakers and only to Manningham, leaning
into the strengthening wind that swept the cloisters, did
it seem unnecessarily long-drawn-out. He dared not leave
his post, and yet he would dearly have liked even a ham
sandwich. Time, however, passed. Twice he was mistaken
by American tourists for an official guide (the good ladies
were dieting) and twice he replied in language the violence
of which surprised even him, and outraged the good ladies
who were after all only in search of Knowledge. And it
was hard for him to appear to be busily occupied *except*
as a guide waiting for tourists; fortunately his gown, collar
and tie made it clear that he was no common felon, for
that matter no common guide either. Once he was spotted
by two of those bristling parents from his desk diary and
had to improvise by blowing his nose heartily several
times and leaning weakly against the wall. For a moment
he was afraid that he had overdone it and that the parents
were coming over to succour him, but in the event they
passed by on the other side. He worried about his health.
He was feeling terribly hungry. Fakirs and people were
supposed to be able to fast for months but they were
foreigners and used to that kind of thing. Three times he
almost gave up, persuading himself that the afternoon
was still young, other opportunities would surely present
themselves, but then he considered that Royalty might
well be persistent, not to say sticky, and his blood and his
brains demanded that he persevere. Once he rang the
bell and begged, yes, almost begged, the housemaid at
least to take a note in to the Headmaster, but she looked
down her nose in a not-you-again way and said:

'We are entertaining.'

At length, at about three o'clock – he was bitterly cold
– his vigil ended but not in the way that a benevolent
fate might have devised. The housemaid, coming out for
air and a feverish cigarette – the Headmaster's wife took

it out rather on the housemaid – looked at him with the contempt that the working classes reserve for down-and-out intellectuals, and said:

'They left hours ago through the garden door.' Then she sniggered nastily. Without waiting for the outburst that he felt to be inevitable, Manningham raced round the edge of Upper Club, where for the insatiable the Twenty-two were playing the Eton Ramblers 2nd Eleven, under the horse-chestnuts and across the Dachet road. The wind was in among them now, tearing the clouds to shreds, sitting on the tops of the trees, bending even the blades of grass. The Guards' band were blowing their cheeks out over the Peers' Entrance from *Iolanthe*, but the wind blasted the notes back into their trumpets and squashed the life out of the music. The umpires kept running in to replace the bails and their white coats flapped around them as if they were struggling in strait-jackets. Off the field of play it had become difficult to recognize anyone, for heads were lowered into the gale and fashionable hats pulled low over fashionable faces. Nobody as yet had seriously considered taking shelter, and in any case there was very little shelter to be taken. Manningham felt certain the royal party would be there, somewhere, braving it, as if viewing the rubble of blitzed London. Thoroughbred faces don't look away when you inquire into them; they look straight back at you, but without interest. Manningham was sailing in a sea of faces; no Royalty, no Headmaster. Sometimes he caught a glimpse of a possible coat-tail and hurried after it to find perhaps a contemplative chauffeur, perhaps only a lost child scalding its iced lolly with wretched tears. I know just how you feel, baby. And then at length he saw them outside the Toilets tent. Or at least he saw the Headmaster smiling graciously after the backs of Royalty who were disappearing one either side of, and into, the tent. Manningham was opportunist too, and seized the Headmaster by the arm. The Headmaster knit his brows (and now he would have to make up his smile again) and demanded waspishly:

'Well, what is it, Manningham? Oh, go away, I don't have time to discuss anything with you now. They may be out of there any minute.' The words were hardly out of his mouth when a particularly violent gust of wind – they could see it shimmering towards them across the grass – took hold of the tent, worried it briefly like a dog a slipper, sucked its guy-ropes out of the ground, and then dropped it as if suddenly bored of a tedious game, and left the canvas there, sinking and sighing, a poor winded thing in its death-throes. From underneath its belly muffled screams and curses emanated, and shapes that could have been Royalty, rose and fell, sort of came and went.

'Now listen, Headmaster,' Manningham was almost electro-magnetic, 'we have a few moments to ourselves. You asked me to report to you if I had any news, and I have. Pemberton's mother—'

'Who?' The Headmaster was exasperated, and his hair was all over his face. His customary pose of mundane cynicism had altogether left him.

'The mother of Pemberton, one of the boys involved in—'

'Oh yes, yes, yes, go on, man.'

'Well she has threatened to expose the whole story unless her son—' crowds were oohing and aahing all around them and a beastly little man in yellowish dungarees kept plucking at the Headmaster's coat – 'unless her son is permitted to stay at the school.'

'Why are you telling me all this now? Oh, really, it's outrageous.' Somebody had got hold of the story that it was Royalty who had been trapped under the canvas, and people were fighting to get hold of the tent-pole. The man in dungarees was hopping up and down as if on a Pogo Stick, and running his hands through his hair. One hoped he was not about to throw a fit.

'Headmaster, just give me the go-ahead to reprieve those boys—'

'Boys?'

'Defries has already gone, of course, and Scarfe, so really—'

'I should have thought, Mr. Manningham, you had enough sense—'

'She's a friend of two of the Fellows; you told me so yourself. She means it.' The tent-pole seemed to have snapped in two, though nobody had heard it go. A young man in a yellow waistcoat took a pipe out of his mouth and opined:

'I should think they might be suffocated under that,' but, generally speaking, a rescue party had been organized, and the canvas was being rolled back quite methodically. The Headmaster was now struggling to get to the centre of the crowd, but Manningham had him by one arm and Yellow Dungarees by the other.

'Just give me your authority, that's all I ask.' Manningham was pleading for his attention.

'All right, all right, do what you like.' The Headmaster swung his arms and his two disciples were thrust away from him. He strode forward, a fine military figure, to the recumbent bodies, just being uncovered, of the stricken Royalty, and the crowds parted for him with a susurration of veneration. In fact, Royalty was neither of them much hurt, but inevitably the dignity of the Crown was silently observed by the majority of the onlookers to have been drastically impaired.

It is to the eternal credit of the British aristocracy, their breeding, their schooling, their tact, their gentlemanliness, and possibly also their sense of humour, that nobody so much as smiled.

It was not until the six o'clock Absence, a more informal ceremony conducted by the individual housemasters in the gardens of their houses, that Manningham had a chance to pass on the good news.

'Will all the members of the Library stay behind after Absence. I should like a word with them.' Pemberton looked at Morgan with raised eyebrows and Phillips's hands flew to his knees. And then Manningham called Absence. It was a duty that he always relished, the short rigmarole of query and acknowledgement, the rhythm of it, the boys ordinarily in their change or half-change with the vari-coloured caps that they doffed when their names were called. Scug-caps, dark blue and black stripes, or light blue and white, faded and torn, worn modestly or aggressively by those who deserved no better, those who didn't have the talent, those who hadn't had the chance, those who argued that games were unimportant; the heretics. And Berwick with his assortment, one day fawn with white crossed racquets, another day light blue and scarlet quarters. There was always a sprinkling of house colours, and this half with pride Manningham saw three caps that were brown with narrow white stripes – Upper Sixpenny. His eye lingered on the less exotic colours of his own garden where he sometimes liked to work for a meditative hour before dinner. The sun was warmer after the turbulence of the afternoon and it glowed with a stained-glass richness on the irises and delphiniums, the anemones and antirrhinums. With remarkable presence of mind, considering, he remembered to omit from the house-list the names of Defries and Scarfe. It was better that there should be the minimum of gossip for the moment. There would be time enough in a day or two for the edited story to be put about. It always amused him to hear the shrill replies of the last half-dozen names and then the deep grunt of Macready whose voice had broken early. Well, now for it. There were no more names on the list.

'You four,' they none of them looked nervous except Phillips, who was picking at the cardboard in the peak of his Scugger, 'the Headmaster and I have decided to take no further action in this unfortunate affair. I am sure I need not emphasize how lucky you all are to have been treated with such forbearance. You must understand that if the boy had been in any way permanently crippled the responsibility would have been yours just as much as Defries's. It would not have been a pleasant thing to carry through life. As it happens, Scarfe is quite recovered and has gone home for the rest of the half to recuperate. You, Phillips, as the one least to blame because least experienced, will take over Defries's Captaincy of the House, although you understand I shall have to limit your authority, and I should like to see you tomorrow to discuss any special problems that may arise in this connexion. In the meantime, I must ask you all to be discreet. All right, you may go now.' They none of them did. 'I said you may go, the incident is closed.' They all went. Morgan turned once and looked into the eyes of the housemaster with an I-know-just-how-you're-feeling-old-man expression, to which Manningham had no answer. However, he picked himself a rambler rose for his buttonhole and went indoors.

The names of the boats in the two Fourth of June processions are noble names redolent of history that roll off the tongue like cannon-balls. *Prince of Wales*, *Victory*, *Britannia*, *Thetis*, *Defiance*; one understands why England is a bulwark against infection – though she has some pretty diseases of her own brewing – and the hand of war. *Hibernia*, *Alexandra*, *St. George*, *Dreadnought* and the noble, ten-oared *Monarch*; as one hears the names one sees Drake at bowls on Plymouth Hoe, and the thick-legged Holbein Henry smashing tennis balls into the gallery at Hampton Court. Well, some of us do.

The first Procession of Boats at six-thirty is little more than a dress rehearsal; those with friends or relations in the Boats, those eager for the best situations along the river-bank, those inexpressibly and inexplicably hungry for the creaking of a rowlock or the dripping of a feathered oar, those enviable ones with too much time to spare, hurry through Weston's Yard, Luxmoore's Garden, or over Sheep's Bridge towards Fellows' Eyot. Others take their time. But the cox of the *Monarch* learns how it feels to have been an admiral, and the oarsmen in their Fourth of June Boaters learn how it feels to have been at Winchester, and the other coxes, a little self-conscious, perhaps almost flirtatious, with their posies, learn how it feels to have been a bridesmaid.

And the river turns from syrup to treacle. And the sky from flame-orange to lemon-yellow. And a swan flies into the sun, and that's a sight to make anyone cry out with the goddamn beauty of it. And the buffeted, weary crowd slips the catch on its last picnic hamper, and there is coffee in thermoses now, or hot rum-punch for those with the sea in their blood or any other excuse. Pretty little sisters are disproportionately worried that the high wind will carry the rockets away out of sight, or if not out of sight, at least behind the tree. Jill doesn't worry about that; all day she has been concerned about other things. Since Phillips's awful assault that morning she has been subdued and silent, trotting along obediently enough behind Phillips and her brother, who had joined them for lunch, and smiling abstractedly whenever she thought a

smile was required. Even Roderick, whose sensibilities
were about as tender as a chewed-over steak, noticed
that something was wrong and offered her a penny for
her thoughts. She managed a smile: 'Don't waste your
money.' But Phillips was his usual self and seemed not to
have given the incident a second thought. He had not
been extravagantly brilliant company, was seldom that,
but had been informative and amusing enough and even
quite thoughtful at times. At tea in his room, just before
he ran off for Absence (the bed was still down and the
brother had plunked himself upon it, so that was that),
he had asked her:

'Would you like to – er – to powder your nose?' and
had shown her where to go. But as soon as he had returned after Absence he had been quite different. Where
before he had been thoughtful, he was solicitous, where
he had been polite, he was amusing. He showed them
where he had burnt his initials in the wall with his poker
and how in his sock-cupboard he kept a box of Penguins
and ate them one a day in Chambers and was able to
tell at a glance by a system of piles how many days were
left till Long Leave. He had told them the funny story
about the witch doctor and entertained them with his
imitation of his Classical tutor. Now waiting for the boats
opposite Fellows' Eyot, with the rather dim outline of the
Sun God, if not in a different constellation, at least on
a different rug, he had taken Jill's unprotesting hand and
chafed it into warmth, so vigorously that she was forced
to cry out in spite of her determination not to. And then
he had drawn it to his lips and, almost intuitively, turned
it and kissed it on the palm where it was always moist and
white. Jill had trembled a little because the wind was
growing cold around them. Then he had held it tightly
while they waited, and Jill had turned to him with a look
of wonder shining in her eyes.

7*

'Poor hand,' she had said, 'what a lot it has to put up with!'

Then a little later as the boats were rowed upstream, he had had to spoil it all again. It was now as dark as it would ever get – literally speaking – and he gently drew the same hand down between his legs, and pressed his knees and his thighs tightly together. Now it may be that Jill entirely misunderstood his motives or was afraid of what her brother might see or was afraid of herself or was afraid of Phillips or was afraid of the whole terrifying world, because she took her hand away again at once and almost sobbed:

'No, no. You don't understand. You *don't*.' And it was true that he didn't understand (understand what?), because he had not been thinking of her at all, but of something he had heard Pemberton tell Morgan After Twelve a few weeks ago.

God damn and blast my mother, thought Berwick bitterly, where the hell was she now? It was horrible. He could never have imagined that the Fourth could have been so horrible. In spite of what Manningham had said after Absence, and looking back on it Berwick had never really believed in those threats of Manningham's, he felt almost ready to shoot himself. Beatrice, of course, was the trouble. Beatrice before lunch he could take; that was a matter only of keeping his end up. He had no duty, as he saw it, to keep the old bitch amused. For Heaven knows why his mother had brought her over unless it was to keep him happy while she went gallivanting off with – well, with whom? Keep him happy with that – that soul of middle-class respectabil – Oh God, just look at her now! Beatrice was dancing up and down on the river-bank with her skirt tucked under like bloomers, singing:

'Call me early in the morning, mother,
For I'm to be queen of the may.'

Oh God. It was the champers, of course. Before it had
been: 'I wonder if you'd be kind enough to excuse me
for a moment,' and 'The weather's improving a little, I
should imagine, wouldn't you?' But then at lunch like
an idiot he had unwound the wire and – pop! – she too
had blown her top. Well, his name would be mud, he'd
been resigned to that for some hours now. Everyone had
seen them, must've. Everyone who counted for anything
at all. People in Pop. With her prancing and singing
and staggering and even, till he thrust it off, an arm
round his shoulder the whole length of Common Lane.
Oh God.

The *Defiance* came drifting downstream, all eight
oarsmen standing up behind their upright oars, the
fragile canvas shell rocking slightly on the corrugated
surface of the river. There would be swampings tonight.
Beatrice had quietened a little now and was singing softly
to herself:

'Little man you're crying,
I know why you're blue;
Someone took your kiddycar away.
Better go to sleep now,
Little man you've had a busy day.'

Other boats came floating down, the oarsmen standing
up in pairs, at the cox's restrained orders, as if sound
waves could capsize the boat, from the middle. To cheers
and cat-calls and a murmuration of anxiety from the
mothers in the crowd, who were motherly and wishful in
about equal and therefore schizophrenic proportions, the
Thetis wobbled with increasing violence. All eyes were on

the tremblement of the rudder, which was the significant clue to the urgency of the danger. A midshipman with brass buttons and a bouquet of sweet peas, the cox, bent at the knees, but he mustn't sit down now. Now! Now! Now! Eight oarsmen and eight oars tilted and fell in a welter of wood and flesh and water and cries; the cox dived for it. The spectators loved it. The mothers wanted to. The river expected it and exacted it. A posy of sweet peas was swept downstream to sink long before it reached London Bridge.

Beatrice was asleep, head on her arm like a child or a dog or a passenger in an aeroplane, and her hair was stuck to her forehead in disarray. She looked pretty sick. Berwick stared down at her and hated her; hated all women, and his mother with them, and realized that he never wanted to see one or speak to one again.

It was a phase he had to go through.

For all her faults, Alethea Berwick, when she gave someone her word, was true as oak. Especially if it was a man. And that morning she had given her word to Manningham who was, to all intents and purposes, a man. And the fact that her intents and purposes coincided so nearly with his meant that neither of them now needed to waste any time on polite backchat. However, a man of perfect celibacy (whether that celibacy was calculated or not) approaching middle-age may find it rather hard to give way to the desires of the world and the flesh, suddenly, without preamble, after a particularly tiring day, mentally and physically. The world and the flesh were so used to being mortified in Manningham that, in spite of the messages they had been sending him ever since midday, he was not as responsive as he had expected. Alethea, on the other hand, who had only mortified her flesh insofar as diet and corsetry were concerned, had no such problem.

She had blown into the study like something out of Hans Andersen.

'Surprise! Who's surprised? Isn't anybody surprised?' Each syllable sounded as if it had been dragged up with ropes and pulleys from her diaphragm, and badly scraped on the way. 'The little lost lamb has returned to the fold. And how is the big, bad wolf?'

'Inhabiting the fold where it belongs.' At this point Alethea had narrowed her eyes, which was a terrible waste, and inquired about the little lost lamb's lambkin and whether it was still going to be turned out of the fold away from the protection of the big, bad wolf. Manningham began to wish he had ignored the simile, and replied that the Headmaster and he had decided that this was a time for leniency and that Berwick would be remaining at Eton on probation. Alethea had been tremendously enthused to hear this.

'He is such a sensitive boy and has such an appetite for life. So simply sweet to his mother that she doesn't know how she would exist if he had to go to one of those rude barbarian schools up in the mountains somewhere.' Manningham presumed she was not referring to Harrow-on-the-Hill. 'And isn't it a kind wolf to protect a lamb so bravely from the dangerous—' However, she was unable to think what dangerous things, except other wolves, might be prowling outside the fold. So she left the sentence unfinished and far more sinister things than wolves they became, hovering indefinable in mid-air. And underneath their wings she threw her arms around the pedagogue's neck and brought him to her. And as she pressed her famished lips to his, in a passable imitation of genuine feeling, a chance phrase from her pristine adolescence rocketed to her across the time and the place and the sophistication, and she muttered more or less into his tonsils:

'Don't be too hard on me—' She would like to have finished that sentence too, but for the life of her, she was unable to recall his Christian name, though she presumed, with woman's intuition, that he had one. 'Don't be too hard on me, Mr. Wolf.' Manningham shuddered. The books he had read on the subject treated the matter in so much more artistic a way and he was lost for a reply. He couldn't forget that he was a responsible middle-aged man, set in his ways and comfortable in his routine, who was mixing it with a creature from another world, who might do anything to him. It was quite a leap, that leap he had to make from the soft, warm grass at the top of the cliff. He leapt. But it was quite a long time before blessed oblivion (or the next best thing to it) came to his aid and by that time Alethea was on her sixth cigarette and the fireworks were almost done.

The fireworks were almost done. Boys had long since ceased to peer myopically at their programmes in order to be able to misclassify: 'Number Fifteen: A Most Fearful Volley of Crackling Grapeshot amongst which may be perceived Balls of Emerald, Amber and Ruby Fire, the whole Conflagration being Terminated by the Detonation of a Single Thunderous and Fulminous Mortar' and were now, except for the occasional 'Tug' – and there was no accounting for Collegers – content just to sit back and bask in the glow of the 'Aurora Borealis, Scintillatingly represented in a Breath-catching Similitude of Nature's Noblest Handiwork'. The little sisters' fears for the rockets proved unfounded, for the wind was carrying them away from the tree into infinite space and clear air. Towards the end of the display, as each rocket spawned its offspring immodestly in the sky, a tumultuous cry of 'ONE!' rose from the throats of all present; all, that is, who were familiar with tradition. Until at last from one of the yellow offspring (by natural selection, presumably, or because, in art as in life, the yellow proliferate best) came a second starry ejaculation of red balloons, and the crowd thundered: 'TWO!' And the next rocket impregnated the atmosphere with yellow, red and green, and 'THREE!' they yelled. Seven times with a crack that would dislodge avalanches down Windsor High Street, if there were packed snow on Windsor High Street, a rocket pierced the sky and spawned, and each was more prolific than its predecessor. 'SEVEN!' they cried, and seven is a mystical number, but the mystery was how they were able to propagate with such speed and certainty. It was fine pyrotechnique. After the final fecundation a groan went up as the first of the set pieces began to sparkle and crepitate and the Etonian coat of arms with its imperious motto glittered against the sky. And then the face of the Monarch with a magnanimous smile so many times life size sputtered and sparked until it burnt itself out; and then the face fell apart as if rotten or leprous, and the chin and the nose and the part of the forehead fell to the ground, and then the whole edifice tottered and blazed and fell, and the whole glorious thing was revealed for what it was; a dirty cheat, a façade, a fake. But most of the spectators had already turned away.

CHAPTER TWELVE

AFTER the upheavals of the first month at Manningham's, the rest of the summer half rushed past as easily
and as peacefully as water down a spout. To nobody's
surprise the House was knocked out of the first round of
the House Cup by seven wickets; the new Captain of the
House, who had been omitted from the side by Berwick –
he was omitted from most things now – watched the
conclusion of the match with some satisfaction.

During a heat-wave in July a Field Day was held
somewhere between Sunningdale and Virginia Water by
the Combined Cadet Force, and a strategic hilltop position
was captured five times by different companies making
surprise attacks at thirty-minute intervals up a well-worn
route with First World War rifles and three rounds of
blank ammunition a head. Such achievements should not
go unrecorded in the annals of British military history.
Nor, I suspect, do they. The rough unpleasantness of damp
battledress against the thighs and the sand rising over
the polished rotundity of corps boots. The usual complement of tumbling in the heather. The usual repertory of
Army songs, led by all-knowing, unselfconscious, un-
critical maestros in the back seats of the coach on the
exhilarating return journey. The contortions of that
inexhaustible pair, Deadeye Dick and Eskimo Nell.
Sausages and mash for tea afterwards with the Dame
unbending a little, her heart warmed by the sight of those
fine boys who in so many wars had protected her and her
way of life from the ravaging hordes of barbarian swine.
Oh, they were keen enough when it came down to it.

In the long, light evenings 'knocking about' on Sixpenny or driving golf-balls over the Arches. Banana milk shakes and Canada Dry: 'I'll sock you a bob at Jack's.'

Careworn fifteen-year-olds struggle with their examination papers at Early School, writing short paragraphs about the Treaty of Ryswick or Dr. Sacheverell, wondering 'If you were not British what nationality would you prefer and why?', translating: 'Tum Seneca gloriae eius non adversus . . .' or 'τμσοῦτο τι πλῆθος αὐτῶν εἶναι . . .' And at night with the curtains drawn, writing short paragraphs in their diaries – the ones who cared – about religion and sex, wondering what would become of them if they went on like this, and translating themselves in their dreams into heroes, fighters, men.

Berwick prospered. The picture of him and his fancy woman parading down Common Lane had caught the public imagination and he was elected to Pop on the strength of it. He played for Second Upper Club whenever his fans could get him to. At other times, and particularly After Twelve, he could be found in Tap, pretending to be drunk on weak beer and using Christian names like a real man of the world.

Morgan and Pemberton went their own sweet and sour ways. For them the afternoons were long for they were both 'slack-bobs'. They swam sometimes at Athens, or lay in the sun together in the long grass with the sharp edges and the seeds that stuck to their clothes, hardly talking. And they would sleep out their sleep and Pemberton would wake up, wash off his drowsiness in the river, and want to discuss things that mattered, and Morgan would let him, not moving, except to brush off a mosquito or the perspiration from his eyes. Then suddenly Pemberton would have committed himself too deeply to an extreme opinion which he had never meant to express, and Morgan would turn Pemberton's silliness back into him like a knife. And, when Morgan had finished playing with Pemberton's mind, dislodging what was ingrained, blunting what was clear-cut, and insinuating disturbing notions about right and wrong, morality and necessity, conscience and conscientiousness, he would sometimes play with Pemberton's body, but in an idle disinterested way. And Pemberton became more and more hypnotized by the power of the other's personality, and Morgan became more and more bored, more and more arrogant, older and older in a callow world.

For Manningham himself June and July were disturbing months. He was kept outrageously busy. To add to his ordinary duties, the running of the house, the teaching of his divisions, the presiding at Pupil Room, meals, Absence and Prayers, the holding of 'Private Business', the attending of staff meetings, the comprehensive nocturnal rounds, the preparation of Order Cards, the signing of exeats, 'rips' and 'tickets', he had now to take upon himself the additional duties of house discipline; for the Headmaster had insisted that the Library must for the remainder of the half be no more than a shell or a husk of a Library, with fags, but without the power to punish them; with authority only to impose fines by way of discipline (and with an official accountant – Manningham – to check that the money found its way into the Eton Mission box). Berwick in disgust sat on the Tschaikovsky record. But the Headmaster had behaved generously since the upheaval. He had approached Manningham in Chambers openly and unsolicited to remark:

'You did well to hush up that Defries affair. Could have been nasty if the Press had got their hands on that guinea-pig boy. Strange how eager the Press Lords are to turn traitor to their own class, whichever class that may be. You know, Manningham, the Press are far more class-conscious than the Public Schools . . .'

That Manningham was so busy, kept his morbid subjectivity and his erotic fantasies (which would not do at all for a housemaster) within bounds. For when Alethea had opened her knees to him in her own instinctively generous way, she had also opened to him the brave new world for which he had been pining these twenty years. And if coitus was a drug, his state of mind – when he had time to have a state of mind – was that of a deprived addict. All the emotions he had repressed for so many years as shameful things, not to be paraded, not to be brought out of their drawer and polished, but to be discarded, ignored, forgotten, flooded back into his mind, so that he was at once philanderer, lover, husband, father; quite a burden for a busy housemaster. Of course some of the time he sentimentalized the affair; and of course he wrote letters to her. Similarly it was as natural that she should ignore his letters, having other affairs with which to occupy herself. But when he was alone and unoccupied (in desk in College Chapel or in the nightly ritual of his bath) he became prey to thoughts troubling and undesirable – though there are those who would disagree – and, even in his sleep, he was haunted by the succubus of Alethea. He went so far one lonely Sabbath night as to cut the pages of the many volumes of Sir Richard Burton's *Thousand and One Nights*, which an eccentric aunt had sent him for his twenty-first birthday so many . . . birthdays ago, and populate the seething harems of Arabia with thinly veiled and provocative Aletheas.

For Phillips his new responsibilities were an empty blessing. Responsibility without the power to bear it and lieutenants who disdained and disliked him made the office of Captain of the House a galling one. In 'Private'

one Sunday morning they had been reading *Richard II*
with Phillips, who had a certain talent for the theatre or
at least for vicarious self-expression, in the title role, when
he came to the lines:

> 'Cover your heads, and mock not flesh and blood
> With solemn reverence: throw away respect,
> Tradition, form, and ceremonious duty,
> For you have but mistook me all this while:
> I live with bread like you, feel want,
> Taste grief, need friends: subjected thus,
> How can you say to me, I am a king?'

He was immediately struck with the personal application of them. He imagined that all their eyes would be
upon him with curiosity to see whether he could bluff away
the parallel with some Gielgud rhetoric, but when, at the
end of the speech, he glanced at them, he saw Berwick
apparently asleep, the others also variously inattentive,
and Manningham himself studying the mouldings on the
ceiling as if he were in the Sistine Chapel. Pemberton,
who was cast as Carlisle, was nibbling at his nose-pickings
and missed his cue. Phillips wondered if he had not been
rather inclined to exaggerate the irony of his situation;
from now on he would throw himself more whole-
heartedly into his duties. And so he began to organize
things, instituted a tennis tournament, and resuscitated
the Debating Society by the radical step of actually
holding a debate. But, domineered by Berwick, Morgan
and Pemberton, and the shade of Defries, this house
merely decided that it had better things to do. And it was
very strange that the house did not respond to Phillips's
Captaincy. One might have thought that, with the
ending of Defries's reign of compromising terror, the new
tyrant would have been welcomed and fêted at every turn.

But not a bit of it. The boys had understood Defries and his methods and they despised Phillips for his weakness, whatever its cause. Even Bigby seemed cold and indefinably insolent towards his new Captain and fag-master.

One afternoon in the curious, unrhythmical lacuna between Long Leave and the end of the half, Phillips retraced his steps to that part of the river where he had met the madwoman with the postcards, and sat on the towpath (it was dry and sunny at last) with his legs drawn up to his chin. He could feel against his knees how the downy post-pubescent hair on his face had begun to harden into bristles and the discovery filled him with excitement and alarm. He waited there for a long time, not sure whether he really did want to meet the woman again or what he would say to her if she did reappear. A few fat holidaymakers in hired skiffs had ventured this far and occasionally a couple of awkward boys – dry-bobs probably – might idle past in a dodger, but for the most part the river was serene and undramatic. If a dead dog floated past – or anything worse – Phillips never saw it. After a couple of hours he strolled back to the Cockpit for egg and chips.

Scarfe had a long recuperation; and a month or so after his attack, his father received a letter from Manningham's Dame, quoting the school doctor's considered opinion that, for a boy of his *nervous* and *sensitive* disposition, a return to the school at any early date might conceivably produce a further hysterical attack and was not in the circumstances honestly advisable. Furthermore, she was sure they would appreciate that so long an absence at this stage of his career must serve to put him behind his contemporaries, an occurrence which, to a boy of Scarfe's *ambitious* temperament, could only result in further depression and anxiety. Therefore, all considered . . .

When Scarfe had recovered from the inevitable depression that followed the attack, his father set him to work in the new broiler house with the calves. Scarfe derived some comfort from caressing these unfortunate animals, but no longer raised his voice against his father's new methods.

Geoffrey Scarfe was making money now hand over glove. So much so that his modest farm was sometimes visited by high-ups with cavalry twill overcoats and gold signet-rings, once even by the Minister himself, who shook hands with him and borrowed his shooting-stick. He was commissioned to do a series of articles for the *Chicken Breeders' Weekly*, and now and then he talked of buying a Jaguar and holidaying abroad. His complexion became whiter and his voice smoother and he started pinching the dairy-maids. He had arrived. His son had not changed much in appearance, though an aunt who visited them on August Bank Holiday was disquieted to notice how his hands were shaking. His parents appeared to notice nothing even when he poured the water at dinner from a glass jug. His voice slowly reverted to dialect, but he always retained a considerate way of speaking to people that those who knew put down to his Eton school days.

And one afternoon in late July to almost everyone's surprise Defries paid them a flying visit. In the full regalia of the regiment of which his father was commanding officer; in an Alvis. And by his side as pretty a girl as any Guards' officer could hope – no, could expect – to lay. Oh, he was a sight for sore eyes! And he gave everyone cigarettes and nips of whisky from the glove compartment. And he winked naughtily at Bigby; and patted Manningham on the back; and even asked after Scarfe, only he had so much to tell everybody that he didn't have time to wait for an answer. And he told them of a funny coincidence. Who should have come to preach in the regimental chapel? Why, the Bishop. The very same broad-shouldered Bishop. Now wasn't that a bloody funny coincidence?

'Bloody funny Bishop!' said Pemberton and they all laughed and Morgan crossed himself piously, almost as if he meant it.

And the summer half wore out like an old blanket until there were hardly enough days left to cover yourself with. And then it was time for the School Concert. Twenty tickets were allotted to the Captain of each house to distribute as he thought best – or found most profitable. For weeks the Eton College Musical Society had been practising their irresistible *pièce de resistance*, a passage from Handel's *Acis and Galatea*, and now on the stage of the School Hall they opened their throats and eulogized the charms of their heroine:

> 'O ruddier than the cherry!
> O sweeter than the berry!
> O nymph, more bright
> Than moonshine night,
> Like kidlings, blithe and merry,'

and quailed at the terrible desperation of Polyphemus:

> 'Torture! Fury! Rage! Despair!
> I cannot, cannot, cannot bear.'

It was superb. And the inevitable Chopin Etude; the audience almost had to duck to avoid the hurtling demi-semi-quavers. Fauré's 'Elégie' was notched on a 'cello and saliva dripped from the ends of flutes. But they were not waiting for these, nor even for the comic duet from *The Yeoman of the Guard*. They were waiting for the School songs. 'The Boating Song.' Morgan and a few others remain either too self-conscious or too superior or too sober to sing, but it's difficult enough not to be carried away by that treacherous rhythm:

> 'Others will fill our places,
>   Dressed in the old light blue;
> We'll recollect our races,
>   We'll to the flag be true
> And youth will be still in our faces
>   When we cheer for an Eton crew.'

Morgan seems strangely moved. But not by the glowing enthusiasm around him. Everyone has linked arms now and is swinging from side to side, each row alternate ways, until School Hall itself seems to be waltzing, but when Pemberton turns to him and scrutinizes him and links arms with him, Morgan looks at him with terrifying venom, and hisses:

'Keep your flipping hands off me, you stupid sod!'

To a roar of applause the four leaving notabilities double up the gangway and take their bound copies of the Vale. Two of them can't sing in tune, but this isn't La Scala, Milan, you know, and a cracked unmusical bass is just the thing to keep the sentimentality within bounds.

> 'What we are leaving, others receiving –
>   New sons of Eton, when we've gone,
> Still forward straining, fresh honour gaining,
>   Keep the torch burning – hand it on.
> Brother with brother, thou our Mother,
>   In thee united thus sing we:

Hearts growing older, love never colder,
Never forgotten, never forgotten
(wait for it!), never forgotten shalt thou be.'

Manningham turns to look at the Headmaster, who is not singing, but is looking about him possessively and proudly. Near him the Lower Master is blubbering away without shame, quite openly. And then the portentous dignity of the *Carmen*, so portentous that the young ones in the audience wait for the dirty Latin word and shout it out (to the intense embarrassment of those sitting with their families). But who could be embarrassed as the final verse rises to its noble and spirit-stirring chorus?

'Donec oras Angliae
Alma lux fovebit,
Floreat Etona!
Floreat! Florebit!'

Phillips's heart is throbbing and he is in love with the world as he strides back down Judy's Passage with Berwick and Pemberton at his side. For this evening at least he is one of them, a real Etonian among Etonians!

Let him flourish! He *will* flourish!

GLOSSARY OF ETONIAN TERMS

ABSENCE : Roll-call.

AFTER TWELVE : Period of work and relaxation between midday and BOYS' DINNER.

BEATING-UP : Beating with a cane by CAPTAIN OF THE HOUSE, Captain of Games, or Senior Member of the Corps within a house.

BILL, 'to be put in the bill' : To find oneself among a number of offenders to be interviewed and probably punished by the Head or Lower Master.

BOY-CALL, a long, drawn-out yell by a member of the LIBRARY. The last fag to arrive runs the errand.

BOYS' DINNER : The boys' main meal taken at 1.30 p.m.

BUMFREEZERS : Short coats worn with the Eton collar and black tie by most boys under the regulation 5ft. 4in. in height. The rest wear tails.

BURNING BUSH : A wrought-iron lamp-post near School Hall.

BURRY : Etonian all-purpose desk with removable top.

CAPTAIN OF THE HOUSE : A boy chosen from the Library by the Housemaster to have authority within the house.

CAPTAIN OF THE SCHOOL : Highest placed COLLEGER on the School List. The position carries official duties

CAPTAIN OF THE OPPIDANS : Highest placed OPPIDAN on the School List. He is the official host for 4th June.

CHAMBERS : The mid-morning break. Also the time when and the place where it takes place.

CHANGE : Sports shirt, sports jacket, grey flannel trousers and a cap.

COLLEGER (Colloq. 'tug') : One of seventy boys who have

won scholarships and elected to live in the original College buildings. They do not pay board and take K.S. (King's Scholar) after their name.

DAME : The woman in charge of health and domestics within a house.

DEBATE : Self-electing sub-prefects with a few fagging privileges but no common room. Supposed to hold debates, but rarely do.

DIVISION : A lesson, a form room, or a class of boys.

DRY-BOB : A boy who elects to play cricket in the summer.

EIGHT : The rowing eight.

EIGHT-TAN, 'to be eight-tanned' : To be beaten by the EIGHT for an offence on the river. Rare.

ELEVEN : The cricket eleven.

ELEVEN-TAN, 'to be eleven-tanned' : To be beaten by the ELEVEN for an offence on the cricket-field. Rare.

ETON COLLEGE CHRONICLE : Weekly newspaper, edited by one COLLEGER and one OPPIDAN.

ETON MISSION : A Mission in Hackney Wick supported by funds from the College.

EXTRA WORK : Work done out of school hours (Technically only mathematical).

FLOGGING : Beating with birch-twigs by the Headmaster or LOWER MASTER.

HALF : Term. Three halves to one whole year.

HALF-CHANGE : Eton suit with sports jacket and cap in place of tail-coat.

HEAD MAN : Headmaster.

LIBRARY : Self-electing, privileged house prefects. Also the common-room where they meet.

LIBRARY FAG : Senior fag whose job it is to keep the LIBRARY in order.

LOCK-UP : The time after which no boy should be outside his house without permission.

LONG LEAVE : The long week-end holiday in the summer and Michaelmas HALVES.

LOWER BOY : A junior boy eligible for fagging.

LOWER CHAPEL : Seats 450 junior boys for whom there is no room in College Chapel.

LOWER MASTER : Assistant to Headmaster. He has jurisdiction over LOWER BOYS.

MESS WITH : Share teas daily with.

MOB : To indulge in horse play.

MOB SOMEBODY UP : To bully somebody.

M'TUTOR'S : My tutor's (housemaster's) house, i.e. My house. Similarly boys refer to M'tutor and M'dame.

ORDER CARD : A fortnightly report which a boy must get signed by Housemaster and Classical Tutor (who may be one and the same person).

P.S. : Penal Servitude. A punishment involving working under the eye of a master.

POP : The Eton Society. A self-electing, highly privileged, gaudily dressed, school society which has no official sanction but does very nicely without it.

POP-TAN : Beating by the members of POP for offences outside the jurisdiction of Captains of Houses. Hence POP-CANE.

PRIVATE BUSINESS (PRIVATE) : Informal discussions, readings, musical recitals, etc., held by a tutor with the Utopian intention of 'broadening the boys' outlook'.

PROVOST : Titular head of College.

PUPIL-ROOM (vulgarly p-hole) : A room for preparation. Hence the AFTER TWELVE preparation for younger boys.

REARS : Lavatories.

RIP : An unsatisfactory piece of work returned with a tear in the top of it. To be signed by both Housemaster and Classical Tutor.

RUN, to take a run: When a master is more than fifteen minutes late for a DIVISION the boys may run to School Office where they are dismissed.

SAP UP: To revise or work overhard. Hence a Sap.

SAYING LESSON: Preparation learnt by rote and recited.

SCUGGER OR SCUG-CAP: Blue and black or blue and white cap worn by all those without athletic distinctions.

SCREWING: Beating with a cane by a Housemaster. Rare.

SIXPENNY: Where the Field Game is played in the winter months and cricket in the summer. Hence the junior cricket clubs, Upper and Lower Sixpenny.

SIXTH FORM: Top ten COLLEGERS and top ten OPPIDANS.

SIXTH FORM CANE: Extra-long cane for use by OPPIDAN Sixth-formers.

SLACK-BOBS: Boy who chooses not to play cricket nor to row during the summer HALF. There are no LOWER BOY Slack-bobs.

SOCK: Food, especially snacks. Hence to sock someone, to treat them to something.

SOCK-CUPBOARD: Cupboard in which SOCK is stored.

SPEECHES: Traditional rhetorical displays by SIXTH FORM. Takes place six times during the winter and once – on the 4th of June – during the summer.

STICK-UPS: Special collars worn with bow ties by privileged boys.

STRAWBERRY MESS: Popular refreshment. Strawberries and ice-cream.

SUNDAY QUESTIONS (SUNDAY QS): Essays on religious subjects to be composed during the week-end.

TAP: A taproom for older boys where mild beer can be bought. In the High Street.

TICKET: Slip of paper handed out in punishment. It bears the nature of the offence and the imposed punishment and must be signed by both the House-master and the Classical Tutor.

TRIALS : End of HALF examinations.

TUG : Colleger.

UP TO, to be up to someone : To be taught by someone.

WET-BOB : Boy who elects to row in the summer HALF.

WHITE TICKET : A TICKET for severe or repeated offences. All the masters whom a boy is UP TO must report themselves satisfied before the boy may again be eligible for leave.